The
Relocation

ELEANOR JANE

authorHOUSE®

AuthorHouse™
1663 Liberty Drive
Bloomington, IN 47403
www.authorhouse.com
Phone: 1 (800) 839-8640

Published by AuthorHouse 06/11/2019

ISBN: 978-1-7283-0744-2 (sc)
ISBN: 978-1-7283-0745-9 (hc)
ISBN: 978-1-7283-0743-5 (e)

Library of Congress Control Number: 2019904102

Dedication

I would like to thank my family, friends and fans for encouraging me to go forth with more writing. Without them, I may still be on my first book. I enjoy coming up with new characters and reacquainting you with the ones you may have already met in previous books.

Chapter 1

Standing in the mud room, Jennifer Jean listened as her mother dispensed the rules to her brother and his friend. It was the same every family holiday! Her mother would decide everything; what the meals would be and when, what everyone would wear, and most importantly, where everyone would be staying, which rooms would best be suited for her married siblings and their children. She loved her large family, their spouses and her nieces and nephew, but she was always pushed aside so they could be comfortable.

Her sister Julia, the eldest, and husband Jake would have the guest room, as mother called it. The guest room had been Julia's old room and had been remodeled when she left for college. Pete, her next eldest brother, and his wife would have Roger's room. Matthew and his fiancé would be in her room, of course. Julia's kids would share the room with her twin brothers. Roger would have the choice of either the living room couch or the basement family room. Since his friend Dennis was spending the Christmas break with them, he would have the other couch.

That would leave Jennifer Jean to find her own sleeping space, again. She had known it was coming, so she had already packed enough things and moved out of her own room. At almost fifteen, Jennifer Jean had been fending for herself for a few years already.

The birth of the twins had come unexpectedly and her parents doted on them completely. To say the twins were spoiled was an understatement. When Jennifer Jean had been the youngest, she enjoyed the title, but was in no way as spoiled as her youngest brothers were. If they saw something they wanted, they would whine or wail and it would be gotten for them. It had become worse as they had gotten to the ripe age of eight. With both of them getting all of the attention, JJ was forgotten most of the time. She couldn't imagine the Christmas presents they would receive. JJ shuddered in disgust.

She shook her head and left the house with an apple and banana, walking across the backyard toward the path through the trees. She had her private space already made up. The only thing missing was more food at this point, but she would slip back into the house later as everyone started to arrive and pack a few more things away to bring out to the tree house. They would be busy in the front and upstairs, so she would grab crackers, meat and cheese, fruit and some bottles of water.

With a private smile, JJ knowing she was always welcome at the Willis' door if she needed anything more substantial. She had become the granddaughter they had never had. They had two sons, but one had gone into the priesthood and the other was killed while serving in the marines. Mr. Willis had found her one day, out at the old treehouse that her dad had started for her elder brothers, but never finished. Mr. Willis had helped her with the last wall and waterproofing the roof. He even ran electricity out to it and brought her a small heater if it would get too cold for her. Mrs. Willis contributed to her hideaway with an extra mattress, old bedding and a small chair. They always invited her in for cookies after school and even meals whenever she was hungry or, as they noticed, forgotten.

Later that day, JJ watched from the edge of the woods as the cars pulled into their drive. It was either now or she would have to wait until way after dark to get supplies from the house. She would have to grab enough snacks for several days and realized she should have started sooner and put a larger stash away. Mr. Willis had given her two old coolers to put things in. He had told her to take them so the critters wouldn't find her goodies and decide to stay. Then he laughed at his own joke. Every now and then, JJ would go out to find that he had filled it with fresh baked cookies and cans of pop.

Slipping quietly in the back and through the mud room, JJ stopped cold in her tracks when Dennis looked up from the island bar where he sat, eating her mother's fresh baked snickerdoodles and reading a sports magazine. He looked over his shoulder to the commotion in the foyer before pushing the plate towards her. JJ took several, eating one and grabbing a zip lock bag for a few more.

"Hi," he said at a whisper. "What are you doing, Jennifer Jean?"

She didn't respond; just slid her back pack from her shoulder and started filling it with food and drinks.

He got up and tugged her pack away asking again, "Jennifer Jean, what are you doing?"

She had no choice but to stop. "Let go!" JJ tugged the strap, but he had a good hold on it. She tried again, "Please, let go!"

"Tell me why you are grabbing food first!" His other hand reached over and caught her upper arm. He was at least three years older, a foot taller, and had fifty pounds or more on her, so he was careful not to hurt her. Men didn't hurt women or anyone smaller than they were, as he was taught by his father and uncles.

Taking a deep breath, JJ looked up at him trying to decide what to say. Looking down the hall she said, "I'm just grabbing some snacks for later. I know mom doesn't allow snacking in between meals." She hoped the white lie worked because she was losing valuable time. She needed to get her things and get back out of the house.

"With the way your mom has baked and cooked all day, there should be more than enough to get you through to the next meal." Dennis was trying for a nonchalant response, but she wasn't buying it.

"Please?" JJ asked again.

There was something in her eyes that tugged at him. He released the bag and let her be. He had been here since early this morning, and this was the first time he had seen her. He had asked Roger where she was, and his comment was 'who cares as long as she leaves us alone'. He glanced at the clock and saw it would be at least an hour before dinner was put on the table, so he would wait until then to make a decision about his friend's youngest sister.

JJ finished off her bag of supplies with a half jar of peanut butter and several slices of bread left in a bag. Merry Christmas, she thought. She looked at the apples, sandwich makings, cheese and crackers, thinking it would do for now, closed the bag and glided out the back door and across the yard into the woods. Dennis was puzzled! He watched as she disappeared from view; he was going to go after her when Roger called him from the front room. Dennis forgot about JJ until dinner.

The dining room was glowing with lights; the chandelier above the table, candles lit on the table itself and the sconces above sideboards along the walls. The sideboards were also loaded with so much food it was surprising they were still standing. There were place settings all around the table with the five kids sitting at a card table in the archway between the dining room and the living room. Everyone took their seats and Roger's dad led the grace. Dennis glanced up and down the table, noticing Jennifer Jean wasn't there. He also noticed there wasn't a place set for her either. He thought this was odd, but being a guest, kept his mouth shut.

After dinner, the family moved into the family room for games. Again, no JJ. No one seemed to look for her or care she was missing. After games were played everyone headed off to bed. Roger had chosen the basement, so Dennis had the couch in the living room along with the Christmas tree. All alone and not tired, he peeked at the tags on the packages under it. He was surprised to find one with his name on it.

Hearing the squeak of the back door, Dennis moved quietly to the kitchen. JJ was standing at the open refridgeerator going through the leftovers. She wasn't at dinner, so he wouldn't say anything negative.

"Hey, Jennifer Jean. Want some help?" His soft voice surprised her and she jumped, turning to glare at him.

"What do you want now?" She murmured. JJ went back to looking at the leftovers. She opened one holding lasagna, setting it on the counter to go back for more. When there were more than enough to make a plate, she spooned items on a plate and slid it into the microwave.

"Jennifer Jean," Dennis started, "Why weren't you at dinner?"

Taking the plate from the microwave, JJ grabbed a fork and started to woof it down. She eyed her brother's friend, gave a shrug but didn't stop woofing down the food.

Gently, Dennis stopped her arm, forcing her to stop eating. "Why wasn't there a place at the table for you?" He could see the hurt in her eyes and felt like a jerk for putting it there. "Hey, slow down before you choke." He took her plate and walked it over to the bar and set it down. He grabbed a glass and poured her a glass of milk. He rummaged around until he found the cookies, and a left-over piece of pie.

"I'll sit with you while you eat. Okay?"

JJ looked at him suspiciously, moved around to her plate and sat down, picking up her fork again.

They carried on light conversation until her dinner plate and her pie plate were empty and a few of the cookies gone. She took her plates and glass to the sink, washed and dried them. They were put back in the cupboard, and grabbing her bag again she headed toward the door without a backward glance to Dennis.

"Hey, where are you going?" He didn't get an answer as he watched her quickly disappear into the woods.

He didn't know what to think; clearly, she was hurt that she hadn't been included in the family dinner, but wouldn't say so. He went back to the living room. Sitting down in the chair nearest to the tree, he started to look, really look, at the packages under the tree. There wasn't a single one for Jennifer Jean. How could that be? There were dozens for each of the twins, several for each niece and nephews, all of the other siblings and the parents. Then the one for him. How could they buy for him and not even for their own daughter and sister?

Dennis was disturbed at the thought that his best friend and his family were doing this to one of their own. Was it something she had done? Was this some kind of cruel punishment? He laid down and tried to sleep, but it didn't come because he was remembering that hurt look in JJ's eyes.

Chapter 2

Dennis waited for her to show in the morning; when she didn't, he went looking for her. Donning his jacket, he took the same path she had taken but couldn't find her. He was good at moving through the woods, loved it actually. He looked for signs of where she could have vanished to. After looking for nearly an hour, he went back to his own house to get a box, then returned to Roger's, tucking the box behind the couch.

The family came downstairs, moving into the living room to open presents. Dennis sat on a chair in the corner, watching, waiting for Jennifer Jean to appear. Again, no sign of her and no one made any comment about her missing. The rest of the day was loud, happy and filled with Christmas joy, although not for Jennifer Jean.

Dennis waited late that night for her to come into the house and she didn't disappoint him. He was waiting in the kitchen this time for her. Again, they talked and he handed her the present he had at home for his sister. It was just a sweater, but it was the only present she got. She was surprised, but opened it and thanked him for the thoughtfulness.

For the next couple of nights, they met in the kitchen. She would get something to eat and he would keep her company while she was there. Somehow, the two of them formed an easy friendship. He asked her what she liked to do other than sneak around at night. She would laugh, tell him how she liked to read, but her favorite thing to do was to draw, sketching this and that; she was learning to do animals and people. She hoped to go into commercial art or be a graphic designer. She also had taught herself how to play guitar. Roger had asked for one, got it and hastily quit playing it once football started.

Dennis told her he would like to go into business, he was good with numbers. Or maybe he would take a look at using his skill at numbers to be an architect or engineer. He still had a lot of options, and his academic scholarship would help him along.

She asked if he was in any activities like sports or something. He responded how he played the three popular sports: football, basketball and baseball. JJ asked if he was any good. He laughed and told her that he thought he was pretty good.

Dennis realized, at some point, that Jennifer Jean didn't really have other friends. She opened up to him in a way no other girl, even ones his own age, had done. Even his male friends didn't get him the way she seemed to understand him. It was strange to have such an in-depth conversation with a girl three or maybe four years younger. He kind of liked it, being able to just talk to her. Jennifer Jean was smart, really smart. She didn't come off as needing to flaunt it, the way others of his age might. She didn't expect anything from him, didn't need to prove anything to him. Dennis was empowered with the knowledge that she felt she could be herself with him.

He asked that if she was home at night, if he could call her to just talk. She said it would be better if she called him, since her parents and brother wouldn't understand their friendship. Over the next few weeks, she would call him at night and they would talk for an hour or so. Dennis even found out she was already taking AP classes in school and was hoping to get ahead by taking more college level classes. She wanted to get out of this town. She had even written a few letters to him and he got a kick out of reading them.

As time went by, not as many of her calls to him were being answered. JJ had no idea why, but figured as a senior, he was just getting really busy with his high school coming to an end. No worries, she would still send the letters. He actually had replied to all of them, so far. She got a thrill out of his letters. In person, he came off as a jock, but his letters showed a different side.

After Christmas, she started to attend the basketball games; she liked the way the school cheered for Dennis. She supposed some of it was for the whole team, but Dennis was the highest scoring player on the team. JJ would watch as her brother would puff his chest, trying to get the attention that came naturally to Dennis. The girls seemed to watch all of the boys, who strutted like peacocks, flirting back.

In the spring, she also went to his baseball games. She would sit where no one would pay her any attention. He was really good, mostly as the pitcher. His bat was hot most games, hitting more homeruns than the other players. Through the spring, he answered only about a quarter of her calls at night, but they would talk a long time when he did.

Soon, it was time for him to get ready for college. He already had his college plans made for this spring, so he gave her his new address after graduation. He was planning on leaving soon after graduation; he wanted to try out for the football team. He made her a promise before he left: she could call him or write anytime and he would be there for her.

JJ took him at his word, but the disappointment came, as usual, from people she should rely on. Soon, her calls weren't taken, messages not returned and the letters were coming back with a carefully written, return to sender, on them. She took that as a sign of an ended friendship.

She moved on, rarely thinking about what started out as lonely a Christmas then, which had turned around into something to remember. She worked at the only way out of her current situation, using the only tools she had: her intelligence and drive to move on. Her grades were exceptional, to the point that the school counselor helped her get into more of those AP classes and even some online college classes. When she graduated high school, she had so many college credits, she would enter college at a junior or better level. With a little financial assistance, she was accepted at a college to start her new life, truly on her own. JJ got her business degree and masters degree within a few short years.

Chapter 3

JJ smiled as she walked into her office at the start of her work day, several years later. The hotel was the newest, and now the biggest in Chicago and she had been here when it opened over a year ago. Her reputation as the best concierge in town had garnered her the job. The owner had recruited her to his new hotel, even before it was completed. She accepted on the spot, since he offered her twice what she was currently making. Mr. Turnquist gave her more consideration than the large chain she had been working for, even after several years of service.

A higher salary, access to the hotel fitness center, pool and spa were just the first perks to be offered. Mr. Turnquist then came with the offer of her own office, not a closet like the old job; a real honest to God office. Mr. Turnquist gave her carte blanche at decorating it the way she wanted. He told her to meet with his decorator, choose colors and furniture which fit her style. JJ did just that!

Having a space big enough for more than a miniscule desk was amazing! JJ's desk now was an executive size, of glass and steel in construction. She liked the sleek lines of it and kept the clutter off it by using in and out boxes; a small, decorative blotter along with her new computer and phone. There were two comfortable chairs in front of it, an elegant credenza behind it and the file cabinet rounded out the office furniture. With space in the corner for a small table and two more chairs, it was a setting for meetings or lunch. JJ was very happy with her work space.

Opening the small closet door, she hung up her jacket, set her purse and briefcase inside before placing her small lunch bag inside the small fridge, which was also tucked inside the space. Going back to her desk, JJ took her appointment book out, looked at the current day's schedule before turning on her computer. Time to begin her day, making the guests happy!

Over the years, JJ had learned it was easier to get people what they requested than to get what she craved. Growing up in a large family had shown her how to cope with wanting, but not always receiving. Instead of going to school for graphic design like she originally desired, she had instead chosen business as a major. Looking into it, she had decided she would be better off with a business degree, where she could make a career move in almost any direction. She took all different facets of business classes, finance and accounting, law and management. JJ had taken a part-time job as a concierge just to make ends meet, but found she really liked it.

JJ had made a habit of getting to know the town, where to get the best deals and the people who could assist her. She knew all the limo drivers and doormen by their first names, as well as the managers of shops where she frequented to get what was needed. JJ knew the owners of clubs and restaurants, as well as the people who took care of the front of the house. She got to know the better-known chefs and sommeliers, florists and candy makers. She had the town at her disposal, so to speak. It was this that made her not just good at her job, but exceptional!

The respect JJ had earned from everyone she worked with was also a feather in her proverbial hat. People generally liked her and she had never heard anything bad from anyone. She knew other concierges in town couldn't say the same thing. They were in it for the pay check, and only the paycheck, not respect. To her, the respect was a testament to her as a person. Money was nice, but pride in her work meant more to her personally.

As her computer came up, she saw she had several emails from the owner, the general manager and even a CEO of a local corporation, all needing something special from her. She smiled and jotted down a priority list of their needs before moving on to the other emails.

She came across one from her friend Michaella and opened it, read through it and answered her with a short note. Michaella was coming into town to work with a new client, had booked a room at her hotel for the next few weeks, as she really didn't know how long she would be in town. She asked if they could get together for lunch one day. Enjoying the thought of her friend in town, JJ made a note to have something special sent up to her room.

With her emails checked, JJ set about organizing her lists for everything which had been requested from the current guests before moving on to the needs of the ones inbound. Lists made, she started on the VIP's, who the owner had mentioned in his email. She smiled as she read his message again. His praises and confidence in her ability to fill the needs of his friends, who were to be guests soon, had made her morning.

With Michaella coming in the day after tomorrow, JJ got up and grabbed her purse, jacket and lunch and left her office. She would head over to the Galleria. It was a little strip mall a few blocks down from the hotel; there were little shops where she would be able to find a little gift for Michaella. She waved to the front desk staff, said hello to the main floor maid and doorman.

The overcast day would have been depressing if she wasn't feeling so good.

During the short walk, she had a feeling that she was being watched. She looked around, trying to see if anyone was watching her. Most of the people on the sidewalk were all walking with what seemed like a purpose, no one seemed to being paying any attention the her. JJ shook off the feeling and walked faster toward her destination. She glanced around again before entering the first store. Still no one seemed to be watching her.

JJ was happy twenty minutes later when she left the store. She had found the perfect gift! It was a glass, purple dancing elephant, twirling a pink umbrella! Michaella would get a kick out of it, she was sure of it. It wasn't anything big or gaudy, just a little trinket to put on her desk or on a shelf. Walking back to the hotel, JJ was more conscience of her surroundings, but that feeling of being watched wasn't there anymore.

Over the next few weeks, JJ had that same feeling of being watched. Knowing for a fact that it wasn't an old boyfriend or something like that, it would only mean one thing. He had found her! She wasn't sure how, but the feeling hadn't gone away, so she would have to start to protect herself, make plans to avoid repeating the past.

Chapter 4

When she was sixteen and needed her birth certificate for her driving class, she had gone to her mom and asked for it. After several requests and her mom still hadn't gotten it for her, JJ went looking for it herself. Her dad kept all of the family papers filed in the office. So late one night, when her parents were out and the twins were in bed, she crept into the office. She pulled open the first drawer of the file cabinet to find the family bill files. The next drawer was for funny things like owner's manuals for appliance and anything new that was purchased. In the bottom drawer, she found all the school files for every one of the kids, clearly labeled.

Looking around the office, she went to the desk and started to open drawers. On the top left side, dad had phone books and miscellaneous magazines. Trying the bottom drawer, JJ found it was locked. Interesting! The right side, top drawer was office supplies like envelopes of several sizes, check blanks. The bottom held more files labeled with specific investment names. JJ looked back at the bottom left drawer.

Locked! So, there had to be a key somewhere. She opened the middle drawer to find a tray with separate little dividers with pens, pencils, clips, stamps and other little items. But in one tray was a key, small and not labeled. Could it be that simple? JJ took the key and looked at the lock. It slipped easily into the lock and turned without any trouble. She looked up, out the office door and pulled the drawer open.

Bingo! Starting in the front, files were neatly labeled, all in order of importance. Wedding info, his name, her mother's name, then each child's name in the order of birth, almost! Her file was not after

Roger's, but after the twins. Figures! Since the twins entered the world, she was pushed to the end of the line for everything.

JJ pulled her file out and opened it up, laying it on the top of the desk. She was stunned to say the least. The first page was the adoption form, then came her real birth certificate and a sealed letter addressed to JJ lay before more papers. She went back to the first page. Adopted? She had been adopted? Well, that certainly explained a lot! She looked at the birth certificate next. There, she found her name wasn't Jennifer Jean at all. She had been named Maria Rosa Giovanni. Her parents' names were listed too. The most surprising thing though was her date of birth. She had always thought her birthday was in May, but in reality, it was six months earlier at the beginning of December. Not only that, the year she was born wasn't what she had been told. It was a year before. Why would her parents have told her it was one date and they had celebrated it then instead of when her real birthday was?

JJ shook her head in disbelief, took the whole folder, closed and locked the drawer. She returned the key to its location in the middle drawer. She went to the door, looked back into the office. Everything seemed to be the way she found it, she turned off the light and left, going back to her room. On her bed, she turned the sealed envelope over in her hands several times before opening it.

Very carefully, she pulled the pages from it. It was a letter from her birth mother to her. Her mother gave her a complete rundown of her family; who they were, where they were from, what business they were in. It explained why she had been put up for adoption. JJ reread the letter one more time. Even at sixteen, she knew what her mother was trying to tell her and how giving her up for adoption was the only way to protect her from a life her mother wanted out of.

She was dazed! The people she knew all her life, trying to fit in with, then being ignored, weren't her real family. No wonder her request for the birth certificate was ignored. They didn't want her to know.

JJ went back to the folder, looked at the adoption papers, her certificate and a letter addressed to the people who adopted Maria. She read it learning more about the situation her mother was in. It was now obvious, her real mother was trying to protect her, by hiding her from her father. But why? Deciding to look into it, JJ would go to the public library in the morning and research more about her real family. Surely it couldn't be as bad as her mother had made it out to be.

JJ looked back at that time in her teenage years now and had no doubt that somehow her father had indeed found her. She wasn't sure how, as she didn't go by her birth name. Her adoption had been sealed, she discovered as she researched her past. JJ had tried to locate her mother once right after she graduated from high school, only to find out she was dead. Her mother had actually died shortly after the adoption; died of mysterious causes, her death was still an open case with the NYPD.

It wasn't hard to find info on her father, as the old papers were splashed with his name and the supposed businesses he was involved with, most were illegal. Sure, he had some legitimate businesses, but the New York state attorney general had been trying to find a way to tie her father to the deaths of a lot of people and the illegal activity in the state.

As soon as she had turned eighteen, JJ had legally changed her name from Jennifer Jean Hanson to JJ Marie Harper. With the name change, her college records were in a new name as were her employment records. She had moved several times too. If she was feeling watched, she wondered who he had paid to find her and why.

JJ had given thought to protecting herself, as her mother had wanted, and the first thing she knew for sure was to have available money. She didn't want to have it all in her name though, so she would ask if Michaella would help her. It was a lot to ask, but at this point, Michaella was the only friend she trusted. Truthfully, Michaella was her only person she called friend. Knowing she would have to give a reason why, gave her pause. If anyone would believe her though, it would be Michaella.

Chapter 5

Michaella came in to her office the day of her arrival. JJ had gotten so lost in her work, she almost forgot.

"Hi JJ," she said, "The front desk staff said I could come on back. Whatever you're working on must be really important to miss my text that I was at the front desk."

JJ got up from her desk and came around to give her friend a hug. She had long since given up with physical contact with people, except Michaella. With her, she felt a kindred spirit.

"Hi," JJ said apologetically, "I'm so sorry! Can you forgive me if I give you a gift?" JJ reached back to pick up the small wrapped box on her desk, handing it to Michaella.

Laughing, Michaella took a step back, "You didn't have to give me something, an apology was enough." She turned the box over before handing it back. "Really, you must have bought this for another friend?"

Shaking her head, JJ looked at her only friend, "Michaella, it really is for you, seriously. I went out to find something as soon as you emailed and said you were coming."

Seeing the hurt in her friend's eyes, Michaella took a seat in front of the desk to open the pretty little box. Once the paper was off, she lifted the lid to find the little trinket inside. Her eyes twinkled and her laughter filled the room. Relieved, JJ joined her on the other chair and they laughed together. They talked for a little while, getting caught up since the last time that Michaella had been in town.

After a while, JJ got up and went back around to the business side of the desk. She straightened up her files, logged off of the computer. Stepping to the closet, she got her jacket and bag.

"Let's go up to your room and talk some more. I have a favor to ask."

Michaella raised a brow but didn't say anything. They walked to the elevators in silence, stepped in and rode up with several other guests to Michaela's floor. She would be staying on the twelfth floor, which was made up of all suites for longer staying guests, facing the park which flanked the river. JJ loved the view from the upper floors of the hotel, and this was the better side in her opinion.

Once in the room, Michaella opened up the conversation JJ dreaded to have. "Okay, spill it JJ. What's wrong?"

JJ walked over to the windows and looked down, gaining a little strength. Taking a deep breath, she turned back to her friend. "Michaella, I've had the feeling lately that I have been followed or that someone is watching me. I have never told anyone this, but I was adopted as a small child. My mother gave me up to protect me from my father. She thought having me adopted, with a sealed adoption, a new name and place to live, might be enough to keep him out of my life. I think it might be my father who is watching me. Or he's having someone else do it."

JJ stopped at the point to see how Michaella took this information. "So, why would your mother want to hide you from your father? Have you tried to find her to ask her?"

"My mother is dead."

Michaella was now shocked. "I'm sorry JJ." She got up from her chair to go to hug her friend. "Why don't you start at the beginning and we'll work through this?"

They went over to the sofa and sat together. JJ started at the beginning, telling Michaella of her life before she found the adoption papers. JJ had never confronted her adoptive family about the adoption; she didn't see the point. She talked about how she had tried to locate her mom, only to find she had died. She had dug into who her father was, what he did and how the New York district attorney had tried to build a solid case against him. JJ told Michaella how she had changed her name when she turned eighteen and started college under the new name.

Michaella took it all in, letting JJ get it all out. When it seemed like she had told all of the story, an amazing movie type of story, Michaella started with light questions.

"Tell me, when was the first time you felt you were being watched?"

JJ had to think about it, she wondered if the first time really was the day at the mall? She mentioned that day and the few times after that.

"Michaella, I need your help! It's nothing illegal or anything." JJ paused, she got up and started pacing. "I think I should start to prepare to hide from him, and to do that I need to have available money, which is easily accessible. I have done some research at a few banks around here. If I opened an account or have a friend open it, I can be a signee on the account and still have access to the money. Since it's not technically in my name, he wouldn't know it existed and he wouldn't be able to locate me. I would move money into it from my current account and have a deduction added to it from my current pay. Then, should I feel it necessary to disappear, I would have a nest egg to do it with."

"So, what you want, is for me to open the account for you?" Michaella was okay with this, she knew JJ didn't have a lot of friends, and none that she really trusted. She had told Michaella as much just by telling her this incredible story. "JJ, what bank do you want to use?"

Stunned, JJ sat down in the nearest chair. Michaella believed her and was willing to help.

"I thought one in Madison, where you live. You can open it when you get home and send me a bank card to sign. I can get you the opening deposit in a day or two." Concerned that she might be putting her friend in danger, she had to ask again. "Are you sure Michaella? I don't know what he is like and don't want to put you in any danger because of me?"

"I am more than sure. You're my friend and I want to help. What you're asking isn't all that big of a deal." Michaella laughed, "I am actually pretty good at hiding money. If I didn't, Eric would spend every cent."

JJ knew about Michaella's husband, Eric. They had many conversations about him and his inability to get a job or hold one. JJ felt bad for Michaella, to have to be the one who supported the two of them.

Wanting to lighten the mood, JJ suggested they go out for drinks and an early dinner. She knew just the place, where the margaritas were bottomless and the Mexican authentic. Michaella laughed, grabbed her purse and gestured toward the door.

"Lead the way! We'll seal the deal over a drink."

Several weeks later, JJ got the bank account number and signature card in the mail. She immediately signed it and returned it to Michaella's bank. With the account number in hand, she went to the HR office and asked to change her deductions on her paycheck. She added more going to her own savings account, then at her bank had a transfer sent to the new account. Now, she felt better, having a solid start on hidden funds.

Over the next few months, JJ still had the feeling of being watched. It always happened when she was out in public though, never at her apartment or within the hotel. The hairs on the back of her neck always seems to tingle as soon as she would leave the hotel. It would only last while she was on the street and would disappear if she went into a store or shop. She would get the feeling on and off, several times a week, then nothing again for a few more weeks. JJ wasn't sure who the person doing the watching was, since she never seemed to recognize anyone. She was sure though, that at some point, he would make himself known.

Chapter 6

Over a year later, JJ returned to her office after a very stressful meeting. She stopped in her tracks as soon as she was over the threshold. There were two men standing in her office, one looking out the window and a second standing back against the wall. The one at the window was older, dressed impeccably in a high-end suit and shoes. The one by the wall, was also in a suit, but nowhere near the cost of the elder man. They were both good looking men and knew it.

"Good afternoon, gentlemen. May I help you?" JJ said coolly. She wasn't happy to have anyone in her office, especially someone who wasn't invited. She would have a conversation with the other staff of the hotel and security to find out who allowed it to happen, and make sure that it would never happen again.

The one at the window turned and looked her over, from head to toe, which she didn't like one bit. She didn't like the feeling that she might be inadequately dressed when she knew better. She was meticulous in her work attire, her hair and nails. It was necessary for what she did and how she did it. He moved away from the window and came around the front of the desk toward her.

"Maria Rosa, you are the spitting image of your mother. I am Stefano Giovanni, your father."

He extended his hand toward her, which she looked at and dismissed. As it was always the woman's prerogative to take the hand offered or not, she chose at this time to withhold her hand.

JJ walked around to her desk chair, set her portfolio down, and took her chair, looking back at the elder man. He took one of the two chairs, making himself completely at home in her office.

He raised a brow at her and began, "I am here to meet my daughter. I thought it was long past time for me to do so."

JJ was still, she hadn't ever wanted this moment to come, not with knowing what she did know about her mother. Deciding to play dumb she said, "I don't know what you are talking about. My father is Peter Hanson, Sr."

"Ah, so you don't know?" He gave her a quick look, then extended a hand to the man behind him. A thick envelope was removed from the other man's breast pocket and put in the older man's outreached hand. He opened it, producing a copy of her adoption papers, photos of her and her birth mother, and laid them on her desk to view. "I am sorry that I'm the one to bring this news to you. My wife, your mother, put you up for adoption without my consent. At the time, I was angry, but as I cooled down and thought about it, decided that perhaps it was for the best, to keep you hidden from my enemies. But now, it is time that you take your place, your rightful place, by my side."

JJ looked at the papers, and photos he had laid on her desk. Then she looked up at the man sitting in front of her.

"I beg your pardon?" she said. JJ wasn't about to show any emotion, and certainly not any recognition that she knew about him and the adoption.

The determined look in his eyes grew, "I said, it's time that you come home and join your family and join our business."

The disbelief must have shown on her face as she was thinking he was crazy. The time had come to run.

"Maria Rosa, I have big plans for you! You will come back to New York with me and I will see to it that you have everything a member of my family should have." He looked at her again with the assurance that she would be doing as he said.

"I don't know who you are, but I have no intention to go anywhere with you."

"Perhaps, you need to get to know me better. Ask me whatever you want and I will answer all of your questions. Then, we can leave and go back home."

The meeting alert on her phone went off, JJ looked at it briefly before hitting snooze, knowing it would come back on in five minutes.

"If you will excuse me, I have a meeting that I have to be at. If you leave your card, I will contact you when I am not as busy." JJ rose from her chair, picked up her portfolio, a file from the top of her credenza and moved around her desk.

Giovanni also rose, his brow was knitted together showing his irritation at being refused. As she moved beside him, he grabbed her arm.

"You will come with me!" he demanded.

JJ looked down at the hand that was causing pain to her arm, then up to the man's face. "You're hurting me."

The other man she had yet to be introduced to, took a step forward. A quick glare from Giovanni made him step back against the wall again. He released her and stepped into her path toward her door. "I said, you are coming with me back to New York!"

She looked at the quiet man, with a silent plea, "I have a job here, a home here and people I like to be with. I am not leaving! And I am certainly not going anywhere with you!" She moved to go back to her phone to call security.

She didn't see it coming. With a swift open hand, he slapped her across her face; she went down next to her desk. First, she couldn't believe that he had actually hit her. Second, she couldn't believe how much it hurt. She had never been hit before.

It must have shocked him too for he quickly said, "I'm sorry Maria, please forgive me." He didn't look the least bit repentant as she gazed up at him. "I'm sorry," he held a hand out to help her up. "I am so glad to finally meet you, having you with me was just the next step. I will call on you this evening, we'll go to dinner and get to know each other better."

When she didn't take his offered hand, Giovanni walked to the door. "Eight tonight. We'll be by to pick you up. Be ready!" With that said, he opened the door and left.

The silent man shook his head at his boss, then stepped toward JJ. He extended his hand, spoke quietly, "I'm Marco, one of your father's employees." An eyebrow raised in question, wondering if she would accept his help. "Please?" Marco smiled at her, to reassure her that he wouldn't hurt her.

JJ carefully set her hand in his; he helped her up and to her chair. "Do you have some water or something?" As she pointed to the closet, he opened the door and seeing the little fridge, retrieved a cold bottle of water and held it to her cheek. It stung at first, but then started to cool the spot on her face, where her father had hit her.

"He doesn't take no very well, but he's not a bad man." Marco was talking to soothe the beautiful woman, who was still too stunned to say anything in return. "You'll see at dinner tonight, he can be very charming." Marco knelt down in front of her, "Please, don't be angry at him. He has been watching you for a long time, and really needs you to come join him now."

"Why?" It was all that she was able to say.

Marco knew why, but he couldn't bring himself to tell her. Giovanni was going to use his only daughter as a pawn. He had already offered her as a bride to his biggest rival to gain more of the business which was the most prosperous: illegal smuggling. Marco couldn't even imagine what would happen to this beautiful woman. The reputation of Watters was well known; he was brutal and women were just a commodity to him. Watters would use this woman, beating her, forcing drugs and alcohol into her, beat her some more then discard her, like he had done to countless women before her. Making her his bride may only slow the process.

Taking a breath, Marco said, "He has some important changes coming in his business and would like you to be a part of them." It wasn't a complete lie, just not the actual truth.

Seeing her come around a little more was a good sign. Marco stood, "Will you be alright now?" He took a step back. "I have to go, but we'll see you this evening."

She nodded, speechless and still stunned.

Marco gave her another smile, a nod and left to find his employer.

After a few minutes, JJ got up and went to the closet, opened the door and looked at herself in the mirror. The proof of the slap was there on her cheek. She was appalled he actually hit her, the daughter he seemed happy at first to see. There was no way she could go to her meeting now.

JJ went to her computer, opened a new message and made apologies at not being able to attend, asking for a new day to get together. After the message was sent, she opened up a new internet window to check the balance in her local bank account. She was very pleased with the balance! The salary increases and several bonuses had really bumped up her nest egg. She made the decision to move a quarter to her hidden account. JJ would move more tomorrow since she didn't want to throw up any flags, to anyone who might be interested in her accounts. Next, she pulled up the account Michaella started for her. Again, a nice balance, even before the transfer. She would have more than enough to start over.

JJ would hate to leave this city, looking around her office, but there was no way she wouldn't heed her mother's initial effort of hiding her from her father. This afternoon had proved to her, the man who had fathered her, wasn't a nice man to be around. Marco seemed to know something too, something he wasn't willing to share with her. No matter, she wasn't sticking around to find out. As soon as she could, she was hitting the road to disappear.

At seven thirty there was a knock at JJ's door. The man was early! Barely walking in the door herself, she looked briefly at the image on the wall mirror before going to the door. She hadn't even changed out of her work clothes. She had arrived home later than she had wanted, but had a few things which needed her attention before leaving for the night. One thing led to another, and before she knew it, time had slipped completely by.

Looking out the peep hole, she saw Marco standing on the other side of the door. Carefully, she opened the door to him. In his hand, Marco had a large bouquet of flowers, most of which she didn't like. Men! They figured any flowers would do, she thought. At least it could have been a small bunch of something she liked. Politeness had been ingrained in her by her mother, so JJ opened the door to let him in. Before entering though, he offered her the flowers. Graciously, JJ accepted them, taking them to the kitchen to put them in water, hopefully able to cull out the ones she detested.

JJ looked in several cupboards and not finding the vase she wanted, went to reach in a higher cupboard. JJ hadn't heard Marco follow her. He startled her as he reached past her to get the vase on the top shelf. Her height would have made it impossible for her to reach without the step stool she kept folded in the small cupboard next to the refridgeerator.

"Thank you." JJ said meekly. Taking it to the sink, she filled it with water before adding the gaudy bunch of flowers. "Did you pick these out?" She couldn't help but ask.

Marco chuckled, "No, he did. I tried to tell him what you preferred in flowers, but he said that you would like these better."

"How did you know I wouldn't like these?" Being curious was one of the traits she couldn't seem to quench. She fiddled with the stems trying to arrange them, to make the bouquet look better.

Marco actually blushed, "Maria," he paused, looking to the woman arranging ugly flowers, "JJ, he has had me follow you. I watched you abundantly over the last few years. Recently, I've seen you at the flower shop picking up flowers, some for others and some for yourself. I knew which were for you, your smile glowed when you picked your own."

She liked his honesty and shyness, even though what he was doing was wrong.

"Why would he tell you to follow me?" There was that curiosity again, poking its head in to her thoughts again.

Marco stepped away and walked over to the patio door. He took several moments before turning toward JJ to answer. "Your father wanted to make sure you were," he paused. He couldn't look her in the eye, embarrassed. "He wanted to make sure you were still pure."

"Pure?" JJ stopped what she was doing to look at the man across the room. "What do you mean, pure?"

Clearing his throat and blushing, he said quietly, "Uh, he wanted to make sure you were still a virgin."

Not being able to help herself, she laughed, laughed hard, but there was no humor in it.

"Unbelievable, and just how would he or you know this?" JJ was trying to stay calm with this whole matter.

Marco's shyness was almost more than she could handle. He shuffled his feet and walked back out to the living room, looking at her things.

"Marco, answer me."

At her tone, he turned. "Maria, he has known for a very long time, where you were, who your friends were, what you did, where you spent your time." He looked back at the flowers knowing she didn't like them. "We, I mean he, knows about the family you were with, each boy and man you have dated. He had me talk to each one to make sure he hadn't taken more than kisses from you."

Astounded, JJ just stared at the man who worked for her birth father. "Excuse me?"

"I would go to the guys you were dating and have a talk with them, make sure they hadn't touched you in any inappropriate way."

JJ's thoughts went back in time to all of the first dates with never a second. Or the one guy she dated more than a few months and how it had ended, badly with her hurt. She and Jason had gotten really close fast, spending a most of their non-class time together. One day, she had gotten his roommate to open their room so she could decorate for a surprise birthday and she walked in to find Jason having sex with one of her friends, in the kitchen. They hadn't even taken it to his bedroom. She dropped the bags she was carrying, turned and walked out, his roommate trailing her. He said he was sorry, he didn't want her to find out that way. So, he had known Jason was cheating on her, but didn't have the nerve to talk to Jason or tell her. She never saw either again and she hadn't trusted her heart to anyone after that either.

Despising this deception, Marco again turned away, but not before he saw the hurt in this lovely woman's eyes. There was no way he could tell her what he knew; he respected her too much by what he had learned about her over the past years. If he was to be honest, with her and himself, he had probably fallen in love with her. Here was someone who made something from nothing, with no help from anyone. She took pride in her work, herself and her home. He couldn't, wouldn't be part of her father's plans for her. Better for her to hear it from Giovanni. And if they didn't get going, he would be furious with them both.

"JJ, let's go to dinner with your father. You can direct your questions to him directly."

Marco stepped toward her, extending his hand. JJ looked at the hand, then up to the man's face. There was something in his eyes, something almost apologetic, that had her accepting his hand.

He smiled slightly and gave her a nod. They moved toward the door where she picked up her keys, purse and took a coat from the rack. They stepped in the hall, but as she turned to lock her door, Marco slipped the keys free from her hand and locked the door himself.

29

They moved toward the elevator, Marco checking it before holding his hand to the door to keep it open long enough for them both to enter. JJ stepped toward the back wall, leaning against it for support. She tipped her head back and closed her eyes.

"You worked another long day?" Marco commented. "You look really exhausted!"

They really weren't questions, as much as statements. She didn't respond verbally, just gave a quick nod. Riding the rest of the way down in complete silence to the ground floor. Marco assisted her by taking her coat and slipping it over her shoulders, then he stepped forward to open the door before the doorman could.

The limo waiting was running, with the driver standing next to the back door. He opened it as they approached so JJ could enter. Marco looked up and down the street before entering himself. Luckily, they were alone in the back seats. She was relieved, because she wasn't ready to face the horrible man who had a hidden temper and a darker past.

Chapter 7

They pulled up to a large building JJ knew well. She knew the maître de, all of the staff, even the temperamental chef. Making reservations multiple times for her own guests, JJ knew how hard it was to get into the renown, upscale restaurant. Figures, he would bring her here.

John Paul stepped forward, "Miss Harper, it is a great pleasure to see you again." He looked beyond her to Marco. "Did I miss seeing your reservation?" He glanced at his book, checking again for her name.

"No, John Paul, I'm here for a meeting." JJ looked back over her shoulder at Marco.

"Oh, I see," he said curtly. "The name of the person you are meeting?"

John Paul, was a friend, one she could always count on. She didn't want to hurt his feelings, though it wouldn't matter in the near future, as she would be gone and wouldn't likely see him again.

Marco stepped up and gave the name, carefully taking JJ's elbow in the process. John Paul, saw the possessiveness in the move, looked at his book and gave a slight nod.

"Follow me please!" He moved through the busy restaurant, taking them to a small secluded meeting room in the back of the house. He opened the door and stepped aside to let them enter ahead of him.

When she had stepped in, JJ saw her father sitting alone at the table set for only two. So, Marco wasn't welcome at the table with them. Giovanni stood, moving around the table and held the chair across from where he had been sitting. Having no choice, JJ took the seat.

Marco took a spot against the wall behind his boss, watching her with an expression JJ thought was regret. JJ wondered if he wasn't happy to see her here either. Again, she had the feeling he knew something he didn't like, yet couldn't tell her.

John Paul, doing his duty, took the napkin from the table and gently laid it in her lap. "What may I bring you to drink, Miss JJ?"

Alcohol was out of the question tonight, she wanted a completely clear head. "Just my usual, John Paul, thank you."

The maître de gave her a bow and left the room. He was very good at his job and could sense her apprehension, so didn't question her usual drink of sweetened iced tea.

Giovanni took the champagne from the bucket next to the table. He poured her a flute and refilled his own. Lifting his glass to her, he said, "A toast, to the return of my daughter."

He waited for her to pick up her own flute. Instead, JJ opted for the glass of water, also sitting on the table, making a clear statement of not accepting his toast. Raising it to her lips, she took a small sip, but did not raise it to his, as was usual in the situation. She could tell he didn't like the move, but made no move to challenge her on it.

"I hope you like the restaurant, I've heard many great things about the food and the service here." He stated it in a factual way, trying to keep it from being a formal dinner.

JJ needed to show him that she wasn't impressed without offending him. "I have always enjoyed coming here. The food is some of the finest in the city, prepared by wonderful chefs, the wait staff is very professional and the atmosphere is exceptional." There, she thought, I just showed him that eating here wasn't new for me.

He raised a brow, "Of course, you would know the best places in the city so you could provide opinions to your clients."

She didn't say anything in response. She wasn't in any mood to discuss her work with him. In the back of her mind, she was already mapping out how to leave, so he wouldn't be able to find her ever again.

Giovanni's attitude toward her had changed, like he must have really thought about their first encounter and he would have to modify his approach toward her coming with him.

"I think you will really like all of the restaurants in New York, as well as the shops, museums and theaters. The entertainment venues of New York are second to none. I will enjoy showing you all of them!"

JJ wasn't at all impressed! She had no desire to spend any more time with him than she needed to. This afternoon's meeting was enough to have given her a lesson on voicing her opinions out loud to him. She would let him work at it all he wanted, she just wouldn't tell him as much.

The waitress came with her tea, set it down for her and smiled to both men. JJ knew Sarah, knew she was newly married. JJ also knew Sarah was the best waitress in the house. John Paul had seen to it they had the best, she was sure. Sarah gave them the nightly specials as she also handed each a menu. JJ opened it, but already knew what she would have. She would see what the man across the table would order though.

"Would you like a few minutes, sir?" Sarah asked.

"Yes," was all he said. He was looking at the menu.

JJ stole a glance to Marco who had watched as Sarah left, closing the door behind her. Marco winked at JJ with a friendly smile. Even though Marco worked for the man, she gathered he didn't like Giovanni.

Looking back at the man at the table, JJ wondered really why he chose now to approach her. There had to be a different reason than what he was telling her. Perhaps, she could get Marco on her side and find out more. Unless Giovanni revealed it himself, which she didn't think would happen. He may never tell her; he came across as a man who always held his cards close to the vest.

His voice brought her out of her thoughts, "What do you suggest, dear?"

Stunned, she looked back down at the words, then at him. "You won't be disappointed with anything on the menu." JJ wouldn't give him any more than necessary to get her point across.

He gave her a look, not sure what to make of the statement. "What are you going to order?"

"They have a salad with steak and a raspberry vinaigrette that I like."

Giving her an incredible look, Giovanni said "A salad?" With such a wide range of incredible items on the menu, he wasn't going to see her eat a salad. "Why in the world would you only want a salad? I won't have it. Choose something else!"

JJ looked up at him and felt more than rebellious. If he thought he could command her to do something that she didn't want to do, he had another thought coming. She had been her own person for a very long time, answering to no one. Even her bosses had learned that they could make suggestions, or give their opinions, but JJ always made her own decisions and today would be no different.

"I don't care what you won't have, I want the salad!" JJ gave him a look that said she wasn't backing down.

He sat and looked at her, unbelieving that she had spoken in such a way toward him. People didn't disrespect him and get away with it. Even though they were in a public restaurant, they were still practically alone. He couldn't allow her to think she had gotten away with it now.

"My dear," Giovanni started quietly, working it over in his mind at how to tell her he was displeased. "My dear, I will warn you just this once. Don't disrespect me or challenge my authority, especially in front of my people."

Giving Marco a glance, JJ looked back at her menu putting her own thoughts together. "I was taught that respect was earned, and since you just met me, you haven't done anything yet to earn that respect." JJ now gave his only employee present a direct look before finishing. "As for challenging you in front of your employees, Marco has already seen how much you value me."

Seeing a new expression on her face, Giovanni turned to look at Marco, who had a blank face, not showing how he hated that slap earlier today. Going back to the menu, the man had heard what she had said.

Sarah came back in and stood waiting for their order. Giovanni took one last look at the menu, "We will start with the tuna tartar, moving on with the beer cheese soup and then to the prime rib. I will have the king and the Miss with have the queen, prepared medium, with baked potatoes and sautéed asparagus."

JJ was appalled that he had ordered for her! She had told him she would order for herself.

"Sarah," she looked the waitress directly, "I will have the spring greens salad with the sirloin strips, medium and the raspberry vinaigrette." JJ gave the confused waitress a look to send her off to put their order in and Sarah quickly did just that.

The man across the table made a growling sound in his throat, which never left his mouth. The disappointment was clearly on his face, but he didn't voice it.

Giovanni started peppering her with questions about her work, her employer, the hotel, a lot of general things. JJ answered with short but concise answers, never really giving him a real insight into her real life. After a short time, Sarah came with their first course, or his first course. She watched as he served her some of the tartar. She had never really acquired the taste for the delicacy, so just pushed it around the plate.

Marco gave her a smile to help lighten her mood, but the only thing that could do that would be to leave. JJ didn't dare respond to his flirtations, not knowing how her father might take it. As for her father, he continued talking, persuasively, about the city he lived in.

Sarah brought the next course of soup and a crusty, warm bread, which was actually more to JJ's liking. Spooning some into her mouth, she tried to really enjoy the creamy, cheesy soup. She let her mind wander, answering occasionally when he asked her questions.

For the most part, he came off as a charming man. Although she could never forget nor forgive their initial meeting and the slap she could still feel on her cheek. Nor would she forget her mother's need to protect her, by hiding her.

The door to the room opened once more as the main course was brought in. One of the other male servers carried the laden tray with all of their dishes. Sarah set her plate down first, then his steak. She turned to the large tray to get his potatoes and the condiments, before asking if they needed anything more. JJ politely said no and Giovanni just grunted as he started in to his meal.

Half way through, Giovanni finally directed the conversation back to JJ. "Maria, I am hosting a party this weekend and I will be introducing you to my friends and associates. You won't need anything as I have your room already prepared. I had my personal secretary go shopping to make sure that you would have all of the proper clothing for all the activities we have planned in the few weeks to come."

"Excuse me," JJ said.

"I said you won't need anything. I have everything ready for you." Giovanni pushed his empty plate away, dabbed his mouth with his napkin and looked at her intently. "We will leave in the morning, so you will have a day or two to acclimate yourself to my house and the staff before the festivities begin. It will be a weekend to show off my lovely daughter."

JJ looked at him and knew he was insane. "I just can't take off on the spur of the moment. I have responsibilities here, important people coming in tomorrow and I am expected to see to their needs."

"You will come to New York!" he demanded.

JJ knew she had to think fast, she had to give him something to believe she was willing to compromise with him, so she could work out a way to get away from him. Looking down, she changed her own attitude.

"Sir," JJ started, "if you could give me a month or two, I can possibly work something out with my employer. I could come and spend a little time with you."

The man across the table was trying to hold his temper, since it wouldn't do him any good as he found out this afternoon. "My dear, I just can't wait two months for you to come. I have to have you there this weekend. I have made plans already."

JJ could see his anger grow with her, his neck grew red as did his ears, moving up his face. Any time she could get would be beneficial to her.

"There is no way I could possibly leave without giving my employer notice. I would have to get out of my apartment, cancel my utilities, let alone pack up my things. I need at least six weeks or more."

She must have given him something to think about, as he seemed to consider this change in her response. Giovanni had finally given a nod. "I will give you two weeks! That should be plenty of time to get out of your apartment, quit your job and fly to New York. As I said, you don't need to bring anything, I have everything ready for you."

Considering this, JJ wondered if she could get a plan and get away in two weeks. "Sir, you may have what I need, but I have things that are important to me that I would like to have with me."
Pleading with him stuck in her craw, but she didn't see any other way. "Please, sir, I need more time. Can I at least have four weeks? If I am leaving for good, I would like to do it properly. I am highly respected here and I won't leave quickly without doing it correctly."

The tone of her voice along with the pleading must have finally gotten through to him. "Three weeks then but not a day more. Marco will stay here and help with your move!" With that, Giovanni stood and moved toward the door. Stunned, JJ just stared at the door as it closed. Marco too was surprised himself. Relief flooded JJ; she had a little breathing room, with Giovanni going back to New York without her. She would be able to do what she needed to go into hiding.

Chapter 8

As they rode back to her apartment, JJ worked it over in her mind as to how to ask Marco what was really going on. Since he would still be around, she had some time to find out, but really wanted to know now.

"Marco," she started. When he turned to look at her, she continued. "Marco, if my father has known where I was, why did he wait so long to introduce himself?"

Marco took his time in coming up with the right answer to give her. "First, when your mother took you and put you up for adoption, he was furious. But as time went on, he saw it was a way to protect you. His business and his partners don't always get along and there are hard feelings between a lot of them. Right now, he needs something to boost his standings, and he feels having you there will give him an edge he didn't previously have."

"So, basically, he plans on using me as a pawn?"

Marco knew how smart this woman was and wasn't at all surprised when she had come out and asked exactly what was going on. He just nodded to her.

JJ considered this before asking him, "You don't like your employer, do you?"

Looking her straight in the eye, Marco said, "No!"

"Then why stay working for him?" JJ couldn't imagine working for someone she didn't like.

"It might be hard for you to understand, the dynamics of his business. Even if I wanted to, I can't leave."

The car came to a stop at her apartment building, the rear door opened and Marco got out. Again, he looked up and down the street before offering her his hand to help her out. The doorman opened the door as they approached. Marco went with her up to her apartment, taking her keys out of his pocket to open the door. JJ had been so tired and weary when they left, she hadn't even realized that Marco had kept her keys. He gave her a smile, handed her the keys and said good night.

JJ stepped into her apartment, closed and locked the door. Just because, she looked out the peep hole. Marco gave a nod before walking away. Strange man!

Going into her bedroom, she sat on the bed and took a deep breath of relief. She was glad she was back in her own space. Time to plan, as she looked around the room. It was clear that she would need help if Marco was going to still be around. She didn't know yet if she could trust him, only time would tell her if he could become an ally. She knew for sure she could trust Michaella and from what she had briefly learned of her new man, that would be the first call she would make.

JJ got up and got out of her work clothes, took a quick shower before getting her computer and a tablet of paper. She slipped into bed and opened her computer. As it booted up, she made a quick list on the pad, leaving space for additional notes: work, apartment, utilities, address changes and moving van. Under each heading, she added more specifics to be crossed off. This list was for Marco. Should he happen to ask what he could do, all she would have to show him was that she was actually working on plans to go to the big apple. If it became possible to trust him, Marco could help her. First, she would have to find out if he would keep his loyalty with her father or not.

When she woke the next morning, JJ had gone with her instincts and dialed Michaella. She knew it was early, but she also knew Michaella was an early riser. Relief flowed through her when her call was answered.

"Good morning JJ!" she smiled at the thought of her friend. "What a surprise!"

"Michaella," JJ started, she paused. "Michaella, I hate to call you so early, but," she stopped.

Michaella could hear something in her friend's voice, so she switched the speaker on. "JJ, what's wrong?"

"Michaella, remember when I asked for help last year?"

Giving Paul a worried look, Michaella answered her friend, "Yes. JJ, are you okay?"

It took her friend longer to answer, "Michaella, I hate to ask, but I need your help again."

Michaella recalled why JJ had asked for help before and could only assume one thing. She said, "JJ, did he find you? Was it him who was following you?"

"Michaella, he has known where I have been all along. He has had one of his employees following me lately. He showed up in my office yesterday, demanding that I leave and go back to New York with him. Michaella, I know now why my mother hid me from him."

"JJ, take a breath and relax. We'll help you out, we just need to know how, alright?" Michaella tensed and snuggled closer to Paul, who held her tighter in his arms.

JJ took that breath and started from the beginning, telling Michaella how she had found her father and his muscle man in her office, the conversation and the demand to go back to New York with him. She didn't leave anything out. She told them of the dinner last night and the conversation Giovanni carried on. JJ was glad that she was able to negotiate three weeks; three weeks in which to work on getting away from a man that could be the reason her mother was dead.

JJ ended her tale, telling Michaella that her father had left one of his men to see that JJ was ready and left Chicago within the allotted time frame. She had a suspicion that Marco didn't like what was going on and could possibly help her.

"JJ, hold on for a minute." Michaella said before the phone went silent. She didn't like the silence, but there was no one else she could trust at this point. After several seconds, which seemed like hours, Michaella came back on the phone.

"JJ, we'll be there later today. Paul and his friends will be the movers you hired. I will just be a friend, coincidentally coming for a visit. I, we, won't let you down. Just hold on until we jet there, okay?"

"JJ, this is Paul, Michaella's fiancé. I have the experience and knowledge to handle this. You have to trust me. Can you do that?"

She didn't even have to think about it, "Yes," she said quietly.

"Okay, keep your phone with you," Paul said. "We're on the way." With that the phone went dead.

JJ wasn't sure who Paul was, but if he really was Michaella's fiancé, and she trusted him, so would JJ.

With that call made, she got up and got ready to go to work. Dressing meticulously, JJ packed her things and made her way to the elevator. When the doors opened, JJ wasn't surprised to see Marco standing there. He gave her a smile and held the doors for her to enter, before punching the button for the first floor. In the lobby, he placed a protective hand on her back as they stepped to the main doors, which was opened by the doorman. The limo and driver were waiting at the curb.

It was relatively quiet in the car on the ride to her office, and it was killing JJ to know where her father was and where Marco's loyalties may lie. She decided to get it over with and ask; at least on the issue of her father.

"Marco, am I going to have to see Giovanni today?" JJ asked tentatively.

Marco gave her a sly smile, "No, he is already on his way back to New York." He chuckled, "I saw him off on his private jet. He wasn't happy to be leaving without you, but will stick by his word and give you the three weeks you asked for."

"And I get you as an escort until then?" she said with a genuine smile.

41

"Yea, something like that. I was instructed to make sure that you got everything done so you wouldn't have to come back here."

"There's something you know about me going east. I also got the feeling you don't like it. Would you tell me what it is?"

"JJ, since your father didn't say anything, I don't feel that it is my place to do so."

Digesting his comment, JJ turned to look out the side window. She just had to wait until her friend showed up. They said they would have a plan and she had to believe in them. Until then, she would bide her time and hope Marco would come around to her side. Maybe she should use his apparent infatuation with her to get more answers, not turning him against her father, just helping her instead. She would do her job, pretend to get ready to leave and see how her cards played out.

About mid-morning, JJ got a text from Michaella telling her that they were in the air. She would come to the office after they had landed. JJ responded back with a reply that she could have a room available, but Michaella said not to as there were too many of them and it might be suspicious. Too many? Well, okay, Paul said they would be the movers. How many was many? She signed off and went back to work.

She had nearly forgot that Marco sat across the room reading magazines. Other than leaving once for coffee and lunch for both of them, he stayed quiet and out of the way. She worked on incoming client's needs, took calls and sent off emails. It was a little discomforting to have him in her space, but what could she do? Calling security and have him escorted out had occurred to her, but his loyalty to Giovanni might have Marco calling him right back. That she didn't want. Time, was all she needed at this point. Time and trust that Michaella's friends would be able to get her out of this situation.

As the afternoon pushed on, JJ kept glancing at her phone, waiting for a message that the cavalry had arrived. Just to make things look good, JJ made calls to the apartment manager, the utilities companies and even the service that took care of her cleaning. At each call, she would glance toward Marco, but he gave no indication that he was paying attention to her, but she knew differently. The pages turned a lot slower as her conversations played out. Once she would disconnect a call, the pages would start turning again.

It was time to make the call that would end the best job of her life: to the owner of the hotel. As usual, JJ got Mr. Turnquist's assistant and made an appointment to see him the following day. She then would have to come up with a pliable reason to leave, family emergency matters were the first thing to come mind. If this wasn't an emergency, she didn't know what was! JJ wouldn't elaborate any, just that she would have to leave and didn't know when or if she would be able to return. She hated to lie to the man who had given her so much, but did she really have any choice?

Michaella knocked on her door, surprising both of them, before carefully stepping in. "Am I interrupting something?"

JJ jumped up, going to Michaella and giving her a hug, in relief or support, or both.

"Michaella, what a surprise! Why didn't you call and tell me you were coming to town?" JJ stepped back only slightly, somewhat shy about the show of affection. She wasn't one to let others know how she was feeling.

"It was a last-minute trip and short in nature." Michaella said, shooting a glance toward Marco who had stood the minute she knocked lightly on the door.

JJ didn't want him to become suspicious, "Marco, this is my friend Michaella. Michaella, Marco." She had no idea how to introduce him properly, as she didn't know his full name or title.

Stepping forward, Marco extended his hand, "Pleased to meet you, Michaella." He looked back to JJ and moved toward the door.

"I'll let you talk." With that he was gone. JJ smiled and quickly closed the door.

Michaella quickly sat and filled her in on the plans that were made in the plane on the way east. She told JJ of the other person that came along. It seemed like she had more help than she had expected. They talked more casually for about thirty minutes more before JJ dug for a key to her apartment and scribbled the address down so they could get in before JJ left from work. They would go over the finer details of their plan. Michaella said she would take care of picking up groceries for dinner. JJ stated that she would text before they left the office. So far, Marco hadn't done more than walk her to her door, so he wouldn't know that Michaella and friends awaited inside.

Chapter 9

At half past six that evening, JJ sent a text to Michaella to expect her in about ten minutes. It wasn't really far from the hotel, JJ usually walked it in twenty minutes, but by car it would only take only a small fraction of that. Once that was done, she started to close her office up for the night. Placing files away, she shut her computer down and placed it in her bag. When all was in order, she stood as did Marco. He took her computer bag, opened the closet door for her to retrieve her purse and then let her exit the office ahead of him.

In the foyer of the hotel, JJ spotted one of her clients who stopped her for a quick conversation. Marco was thoughtful enough to not interrupt, stepping way off to the side. Apparently, he had sent for the car while she was packing up as it pulled up while she was talking to the client. When finished, JJ said good evening to the guest and moved to the door, being held by the doorman. The chauffer opened the car door and they slid into the back of it.

"JJ," Marco started, "Would you like to have dinner this evening with me?"

JJ was stunned that he had asked, but knowing that she had people waiting for her, she replied, "Thanks Marco, but I have sorting, organizing and packing to work on." She gave him an apologetic look but didn't back down.

"Okay, maybe we can pick something up and eat at your place?" Marco said meekly, almost embarrassed to ask.

"Marco, I really would rather not. I do have a lot to do and think about. I appreciate the thought though."

He graciously nodded, not pressing the issue any more. There was no way she would let him into her apartment tonight, or any other until she knew she could really trust him. The rest of the short drive was spent in silence. As she had hoped, Marco walked JJ up to her apartment saying he would see her in the morning and to sleep tight.

JJ opened the door, to complete silence. She was almost afraid that Michaella and her friends had changed her minds and left. But once the door was closed and locked, Michaella walked out of the kitchen with a large, handsome man following her. The smells that followed them out made JJ's mouth water.

After an introduction to Paul, they went back to the kitchen where another man stood at the stove, stirring something in a kettle on the stove. He turned as they entered and JJ stopped in her tracks. She would recognize Dennis anywhere, but wondered if he would know who she was.

"Jennifer Jean," he said with a twinkle in his eye. "Well, look at you, all grown up!"

He walked up to her and enveloped her into a hug she felt all the way to her toes. She had stopped thinking about him about as fast as her letters to him were returned, stamped with 'return to sender'. She stiffened immediately; first because of the contact and secondly because he acted like they were old friends, who hadn't seen each other for a few days.

The action wasn't lost on him, he released her stepping back, a frown on his face. "Dinner's ready. Let's eat while it's still hot." Dennis turned to the oven, removing a dish with a mound of meatballs topped spaghetti.

JJ turned, strode to her bedroom, closed the door and leaned against it trying to regain her composure. In all these years, she hadn't seen or heard from the one person who had actually shown her any kind of real friendship, then dropped her cold. She shook it off, went to her dresser to grab some sweats and a hoody, changing quickly out of her work clothes. Taking a deep breath, JJ opened the door and entered her dining room to find the three of them waiting patiently at the table for her. She took the open seat and sat.

In the quiet, Spook said grace before serving them all a more than healthy portion of the steaming pasta dish. JJ watched the interaction between the three people who were here to help her. You could see the deep friendship or brotherhood between the two men. They passed humorous digs back and forth at each other, but nothing that was malicious. To watch Michaella and Paul, you could see the love between the two. JJ found herself envious of the two different friendships, dropping her attention to her plate.

"JJ, are you all right?" Michaella asked quietly. She had reached over and laying her hand on JJ's arm.

With a nod, JJ looked up to see all of them watching her. "Why don't we talk about how to get me out of this mess."

"Okay," Paul started. "Why don't you tell us what you want?"

"I want to disappear and never have that man find me again. I hope I have enough money to do so."

"Alright, let's clear the table and show you what our thoughts toward that goal are." With that, Paul slid his chair back, gave Michaella a quick peck on the lips before taking her plate and his own. Gracefully, he balanced those plates, before picking up JJ's and Dennis' also. Dennis took the salad plates and the empty platter without a trace of spaghetti on it and the plate with bread crumbs on it.

JJ went to stand but Michaella stopped her with a smile and shake of the head. The men took care of the dishes, and bringing dessert and coffee cups back to the table. Michaella got a folder from the side table and opened it as Paul poured coffee all around.

Paul started the explanation, "We have a friend that can make you a new identity. It will be flawless from birth to now. All we need from you are some details and directions from you. Next, is where you would be comfortable going. Michaella, would you like to tell her what you said on the plane?"

"JJ, my grandmother left me her house. With Paul and I getting married, we made the decision to live in his house, leaving my house open." Michaella smiled tenderly at Paul as he took her hand. "You're more than welcome to stay at my house, only a few miles from where Paul and I will be. I would love to have you close, maybe we can work together."

JJ listened, taking it all in. She would hold her objections and agreements until it was all out on the table.

Dennis took up the next step. "JJ, we assumed that you would be packing up and moving your belongings, so Thumper and I will be the movers you hired. We will scope out trucks in the next few days. Once we find two identical ones, we can start planning a route where we can make a swap sending the decoy truck to the east while having your things sent to the west. We thought if they are watching you closely, this would be the best way to throw them off and still get your own things out of Chicago."

Again, JJ said nothing, reserving her thoughts until they were done.

Paul and Dennis exchanged a look, before Dennis continued. "Now, tell us about this guy that brought you home."

Looking around the table, JJ pushed her coffee cup away and reached for her wine glass. After a sip she said, "Marco is one of Giovanni's employees. Giovanni left him here to make sure that I cooperated and left during the allotted three weeks I was given to show up in New York. I have the feeling Marco will be my shadow during the day. He picked me up this morning, stayed in my office all day and drove me home." JJ took a breath, "I hate it, having him there. It makes me feel like a child in detention."

"We'll see what we can find out about Marco and Giovanni. We have the best computer geeks in the business, the resources to put the surveillance back on Marco." Paul asked, "Do you know where he is staying?"

"I have no clue." JJ said. "And I don't really care."

"For now, we want you to act like normal, going to work and keeping any normal schedules that you may have." Dennis was clear in his statement, looking her directly in the eyes. "Thumper and I will do what we need to do about this Marco fella."

All of a sudden, JJ felt completely exhausted and knew she was out of her element. It was clear to her, she had made the right call when asking Michaella for help. Obviously, Michaella didn't have these resources when she first asked for help, but JJ was glad she did now. She had to have some time to think all of this through.

"I really appreciate all that you have done," JJ stated as she stood to step around the table, "I know I couldn't have pulled this off alone. I just want to live my life, not by anyone else's rule. But right now, I need some alone time, time to think."

Dennis and Paul stood too, Paul held Michaella's chair as she stood. "JJ, we are going to do everything we can to make sure you are safe and live that life."

The three moved toward the door, Michaella gave JJ a brief hug before she and Paul opened the door. Paul looked both ways down the hall before they walked out, hand in hand.

Dennis stopped in front of JJ before walking out. "It is really good to see you again Jennifer Jean," he said quietly. Touching her cheek, "I promise, we will get you out of this safely."

She looked up at him; not knowing the man he had become, but remembering the boy he was. The boy who had made her a promise before and didn't keep it. "I won't put money on your promises, if you don't mind. I can't be sure you will keep this one either."

With that she gestured toward the door. Dennis, slightly stunned, stepped out and said good-bye. JJ closed the door and locked it. She truly was fatigued beyond any other busy day. She turned and went to her bed.

Chapter 10

Spook walked down the hall in disbelief at JJ's last statement. When he joined up with Thumper and Michaella at the back door of the apartment building, he stopped, glanced back inside and shook his head. What did she mean by it, he wondered?

"What's up Spook?" Thumper asked his best friend.

"Nothing, I think." He shook his head again. "JJ said something that didn't make sense. She was tired and it must have been fatigue talking."

"I got the impression you two had met before. Want to explain it so we are all on the same page?"

Spook opened the SUV door for Michaella, beating Thumper to it. Giving himself a few more moments to regroup before he got in. "It was a long time ago, she was just a kid then. I was a friend with her brother."

"How much of a kid?" Michaella asked.

"I don't know, I was eighteen. She must have been thirteen or fourteen." Spook stopped to ponder that time during a Christmas long past. "Although, she did seem more mature than that. We connected somehow."

Remembering what JJ had told Michaella she said, "Well, since her adoption family had lied about her birthday, she was probably closer to fifteen or even sixteen. Even though they had never told her, she was almost eighteen months older when they adopted her."

Spook considered that and realized then why they had connected; she was closer in age to him than he had originally thought. She had definitely become a looker! She had grown into

50

a lovely looking woman, poised, confident and he already knew she was intelligent.

"Mic, you've known JJ awhile. Tell me more about her." He looked back at her, directly behind Thumper in the backseat. He was riding shotgun as Thumper was driving.

"She is confident, smart and has paid her dues. JJ started college classes in high school, entering college at nearly a junior level. She holds a master in business, with emphasis in management. She has accumulated a powerful network of business leaders here in Chicago and across the nation just by the traveling of those leaders. She is the best at what she does, and I can say that without bias, since I have also traveled like them." Michaella smiled as she looked back to Dennis. "She doesn't take any shit from anyone either, no matter their size. Until now that is. She is really scared of Giovanni and she doesn't want to be anywhere near him again."

"I remember her as a kid, shy at first, then defiant." He smiled, "Intelligent too. She talked about going to college for art or graphic design. I wonder why she changed her mind." All too soon, he was thinking back to the Christmas so long ago. Knowing what he knew now, that she was adopted may have had a lot to do with the way her family had treated her, even though she didn't know it. He shook his head, still disbelieving in the way they had ignored her during a time especially made for family.

Changing his thoughts back to the present, "Well, we better find out who we are up against and get to work at getting her out of this mess."

They had pulled up to their hotel, parked and went to their respective rooms. Spook pulled out his phone and was dialing Geek as they unlocked their doors.

"Geek, I have a job for you and I need it to happen fast," he said as Spook entered his room closing the door. He went over to the desk and sat down, pulling his computer up. "We have a friend that got messed up with a man called Giovanni, from New York. We need you to find out all you can about him, his associates and enemies as fast as possible." He stopped and listened. JJ had reason to be afraid by the sound of the prelim he was getting from Geek. He stopped his friend's commentary and asked him to compile everything in a file and send it to both him and Thumper.

Then he asked Geek to start working on a new identity and background for JJ. He would get him more specifics tomorrow, but wanted Geek to start laying the ground work for a deep cover for her. There should be no way that anyone could find her, unless she wanted them to and there was no way JJ wanted that to happen.

Spook hung up with Geek and started his computer and started a search for van rentals. He jotted down a couple of numbers with addresses to be checked out tomorrow. Next were uniform rentals. He and Thumper would have to look the part as well. He added those numbers to his list.

Spook's thoughts then went to the goon her father had left to make sure she complied with his wishes. What did she call him? Ah, that's right, Marco. Getting up, he went to one of his bags, dug around until he found what he was looking for: a small tracking device for the vehicle Marco drove.

Next was one for the man himself, he would have to figure out a way to get it on him where it wouldn't be removed every time he changed clothes. While he was at it, he found something for JJ too.

There was no way Dennis would have what happened to Michaella, happen to JJ. This time he wouldn't take no for an answer. He found a pendant with a light purple stone, in a silver setting and chain. Little did anyone know that the setting itself was the small electronic unit with the GPS unit within it. He wondered if one would be enough. He dug around until he came up with one more and something for her phone.

Spook took all the items to his computer, opened the program and enabled the devices, checking to make sure they all worked. Picking up the necklace, he watched as it spun catching the light. The corner of his mouth, turned up a little thinking it would look nice hanging around JJ's pretty neck.

Just like that, memories of a Christmas long past, came back to him. Sitting at the kitchen counter, late at night, talking about their teenage thoughts and dreams. He remembered the ease he had with her, once he broke through her reluctance to be around him, that is. The surprise on her face when he gave her the small gift. He thought of the anger he had at his friend's family as they ignored her. It was something that tore at him still, making it vital that he gave her some of his own time.

To which brought back the comment JJ made as they left her apartment. She didn't trust him to keep his promise. He was sure there was something there he was missing, but couldn't quite put his finger on it. Had he implied something to her all those years ago? When they had more time, he would have to gently probe that thought with her.

The clock on his computer told him it was late. He wanted to be up early and outside of JJ's apartment when this Marco arrived, so he better hit the rack and get some sleep.

JJ's alarm went off just like it did every day for the last few years. The only difference today was that she hadn't really slept last night. She kept turning, trying to find a comfortable position. Trying to get the thoughts of the last two days off her mind. Trying to get over seeing Dennis again had her thinking more than normal at bedtime.

She had heard Paul call him Spook and wondered about it. They had some interesting nicknames. Paul was Thumper and Dennis was Spook. It must be something they had in common. But seeing him again, brought back the hurt and rejection from years past. JJ had never thought that she would ever see him again, let alone have him be someone to help her out of the terrible situation she found herself in. She would take his help only because he was a friend of Michaella's. It didn't mean there would be anything more to it for her.

Turning her head, JJ took one look at the clock and rolled out of bed. She needed to get ready and be out the door before Marco came knocking. She didn't want him to see that she hadn't actually started to sort and pack like she told him she was going to do. JJ knew she was going to have to pack for a completely different reason. Of course, she couldn't let anyone know that. Even thinking it too often, she might let it slip and where might that leave her. It was better off not trusting anyone if she didn't have to.

After showering, she dressed just as carefully as any other day. Today was a pant suit in a fall color of burnt red and a white sleeveless blouse. She had always liked to look professional with clothes that showed off her assets. Though she wasn't nearly as tall as Michaella, she always knew she had an athletic figure. Walking into the kitchen, JJ started her coffee by popping a K cup in the machine, added water and turned it on. She looked in the cupboards and fridge for something easy and fast to eat, but nothing appealed to her. She took her coffee and sat with her computer, to check the news feeds and weather. She moved more of her money to the hidden account after paying her current bills.

The knock on the door brought her back to her senses with a feeling of trepidation. There was only one person that could be. She really wasn't ready to be in Marco's presence because it reminded her of who he worked for and what he was. JJ just had to believe in Michaella and her friends for the help she needed to get out of this situation.

With hesitation, JJ went to the door. She did take the time to look through the peep hole just to make sure it was who she thought it was. Seeing Marco, she carefully unlocked the door and opened it to him.

"Good morning JJ. You look beautiful today." Marco said, smiling at her. In his hand, he held a small bundle of flowers; flowers he knew she would like.

JJ blushed as she accepted the gift from him. "Thank you, Marco, they're beautiful." She graced him with a shy smile before stepping back to let him in.

Marco closed the door, gently as he watched her reaction at the type of flowers she really likes. He walked with her to the kitchen where the others were from the other day. It didn't take him long to pluck them out of the vase. JJ smiled as he dumped them into the trash can. Taking the empty vase to the sink, she rinsed it carefully, added fresh water and assembled the stems in a way to take make them look the best. He stood back and watched and was glad he could bring her a little joy.

When she was satisfied with the way they looked, she stepped back to admire them. JJ turned and smiled back at Marco. They were standing there like smiling fools, acting like they were really friends, when in truth she still didn't trust him because she knew he was hiding something from her.

JJ shook her head. Leaving the kitchen, she went to the table and closed her laptop down, slipped it into her case, gathered her purse and went to the door. In the hall, she waited for him to walk out so she could lock the door. This time, Marco let her lead and walked behind her to the elevator. She entered and looked straight ahead, not showing any emotion whatsoever. Marco stepped in, turned and hit the button for the lobby.

On the street, the limo was again waiting for them. With the driver by the back door, JJ stepped up to the car, but not before she spotted Dennis leaning against the building a little way down the street. She paid him no heed as she entered the car with Marco coming in right behind her. Seated inside JJ was glad that she had seen Dennis, but wondered why.

When they pulled up to the office, Paul was coming out of the hotel as JJ and Marco entered. She nearly didn't recognize the man as he was dressed in an expensive suit, glasses and carrying a briefcase. Like when she saw Dennis, she gave no indication that she knew him.

JJ said hello to the doorman, bellhop and the front desk attendant before heading to her office. Going on habit, she moved around her office getting ready for her day; purse in the closet, computer on desk, water the plant. She completely ignored Marco. Even if he was nice and courteous to her, he was still withholding something from her.

Chapter 11

The day crept by, it was really hard to pretend to be busy when someone was sitting there pretending not to be watching her. She had to give Marco credit though, he never interfered with her work. People came and went, calls came in and appointments were kept. Any outsider wouldn't know she was planning on leaving, that her work here was coming to an end. That thought saddened her, because she had made something of herself here in this position.

Late in the afternoon, JJ got an email from Michaella asking to meet her for dinner, naming the restaurant and time. Now, she had to figure out a way to get there without Marco tagging along. Just how was she going to accomplish that? She spent the next half hour thinking about it. Then her chance came.

"JJ, it's about quitting time," Marco said. "Why don't we go out for dinner?"

"Actually, Michaella's meetings went longer than she expected and she is still in town. She would like to have dinner with me. You don't mind, do you?"

The disappointed look he gave her said it all. He did have feelings for her! Maybe in a different time or place a relationship between the two of them might have been possible. But the fact that she knew he was withholding something from her, prevented her from ever trusting him. If she could get him to tell her, perhaps things could change her feelings for him.

"No, that's fine. Can I drop you off? Would you like me to come back and pick you up and take you home?"

"That won't be necessary. I don't want to put you out, I can grab a cab and Michaella can give me a ride home." JJ felt compelled to say something more. "Marco, I can tell that you care for me, so why won't you tell me what you are hiding about my father's plans for me?"

Marco swallowed, looked anywhere but at JJ. "JJ, I," then he stopped. He took a few seconds, "JJ, I do care about you and I will do everything in my power to protect you. Even from your father, should it come to that. But for now, I am going to do my job and see that you go to him in New York."

Not knowing what to reply to him, JJ started to close down her computer, clean her desk and gather her things to leave for the day.

He took her computer, "Please let me take you to meet your friend."

Her only response was a quick nod, before leaving her office.

When they left the hotel, the car was waiting for them. True to his word, Marco saw her to the restaurant. The driver pulled up, Marco got out and helped her out of the car. He walked her through to the host station and almost walked her to the table. With only a look, JJ stopped him from going beyond the desk.

JJ told the hostess Michaella's name and was shown to the table. Marco watched as the two women hugged, then the man at the table stood and also gave her a hug. Marco had never been jealous before and didn't like how it felt. He had told JJ the truth about protecting her. If this was someone he needed to remove from her life, he would do it and wouldn't have second thoughts about it. He was relieved to see Michaella and the man hug and there was a look between the two which said they were together. As they sat back down, Marco took one last look before leaving. He was getting into the car when Spook came and sat down at the table.

Michaella was happy to see JJ, but not to see she had been escorted by Marco. She had seen him and had the foresight to ask Dennis to step away from the table in case he did come all the way over to them. She saw Marco leave and waved Dennis back over to the table. Once they had all seated, Michaella could see JJ visibly relax. Time to keep the conversation light and away from JJ's troubles.

"JJ, will you be a bridesmaid at our wedding? My friend Lauren will be my maid of honor. We're going to keep our wedding party small. Belinda, one of Paul's friends is an event planner. She's offered to help us with all of the planning."

JJ was flattered to be asked. Quietly, she gave her answer, "Yes, I would be honored." She had never had a friend close enough to her to be asked such a personal question. Shyness took over and she looked down at her place setting.

Her reaction wasn't lost on the others at the table. Dennis took her reaction in, remembering her from last night and then again years ago. Last night she was hesitant, guarded, almost anxious. She wasn't comfortable with them in her space. Years ago, she was mostly defiant and hurt. He wanted to see her happy, he realized. To do that, she would have to be safe from her father.

They had gotten the report today from Geek about her birth father and it was even worse than she had told them. Giovanni had been indicted multiple times by the state and federal governments, yet had never actually gone to trial. He was dirty and played dirty, making evidence and witnesses disappear. It was very possible that he had some law enforcement officials in his pocket too. JJ was right to want to hide from him and could only accomplish that with their help.

Dennis looked her over in her suit of a different color red than he had ever seen. The white shirt gave her skin a darker glow. Desire flashed through him as he looked at her, thinking about stripping her down to bare skin. Cleaning his thoughts, he shifted in his chair and looked at the menu their waitress had handed out. When he looked up, JJ was staring at him. He wondered what was going through her mind.

JJ looked to her left, at the man Dennis had become. She was unsettled last night at seeing him after all of these years, and even more so tonight. She knew she had changed and wondered about him. He had been so easy to talk to years ago. Could she find that with him again? Only time would tell.

"JJ," Dennis said bringing her out of her thoughts. "The waitress is ready for your order. Do you know what you would like?"

JJ blinked at Dennis, then looked up at their waitress. She gave her order then taking her glass of water, took a healthy drink.

The evening was pleasant, the conversation was light and completely stayed away from the future. They joked, laughed and JJ even flirted with Dennis. When the time came, they left the restaurant, but not before Dennis checked the whereabouts of Marco and his car and driver. When he was sure they weren't outside, he stepped out to make a visual assessment. He signaled for the valet to bring their SUV up. Coming back in, he gave Paul some kind of sign and they all walked out together. Dennis opened the door for JJ even as he looked around, just as Marco had done. Paul followed suit, doing the same for Michaella. They went back to JJ's apartment before starting on the more serious business of getting her away, free and clear.

Being the hostess, JJ got everyone something to drink as they sat around her living room. She hadn't noticed the duffle Dennis brought with him into the building,.which he opened it to reveal a sleek looking computer, along with some other tech devices she knew nothing about. Quickly, he brought up a file then pushed it across her coffee table to JJ.

"We dug a little deeper on your father. I think that you should really know what we're up against. He is not a kind or gentle man, JJ. The sooner we get you out of here, the better it will be. I have our computer guru waiting for a few more vital statistics on you to complete your new identity."

JJ looked down at the computer, at seeing how large the file was, she shut the lid. Rubbing her cheek, she said, "You don't have to tell me the kind of man he is. And I don't need to look at any file on him either." JJ stood and paced her small living room, coming to stop in front of her bookshelf, "I just want away from him and as soon as possible."

Dennis watched her, noticing she stayed away from the picture window, and realized for the first time that she really was scared. He could also tell she didn't like the feeling. Cool, composed, in control, that was the way she ran her life. He saw the her rub her head again and would ask her about it later.

Paul picked up the conversation from there. "We have two identical trucks rented out and can start loading any time." He looked to Michaella and Dennis before moving on. "We have a few thoughts on getting Marco out of the way, that is, if we can't get him on your side."

Without turning, JJ said, "What do you need for the identity information?"

It was Paul who said what was needed with Michaella taking swift notes as JJ recited her answers. She wasn't opening up to anyone at all, which Michaella found odd. Was it just the men or was it because of the situation she was in? Past experience told Michaella how JJ was warm and big hearted, had a great sense of humor and could keep you laughing. She looked really tired today too. Maybe it was time for them to call it a day.

Michaella nudged Paul with a nod toward the door. He got the clue and stood, helping her up. "JJ, we will take off now and talk more tomorrow." Quietly, he ushered Michaella out, but not before he gave Spook a look. Being friends a long time, it was easily interpreted as be careful.

Dennis could tell that JJ didn't really hear them leave, since she was so deep in thought. He continued to watch her, appreciating what he saw too. Not really sure why he was doing it, Dennis got up to move around the room to where she was standing. He took her in his arms and just held her. She stiffened at first and tried to pull away. Friendship was a tenuous balance between trust and respect, she needed both from him, for him to help her. He would wait until she was comfortable with him before he let her go.

Unaccustomed to being touched, JJ took a deep breath hoping he would let her go, and soon. Never having a boyfriend, or girlfriend for that matter, the only physical contact she normally had was a business handshake. Her family had been close with each other, but never with her. The boys wrestled with each other, her mother would hug her brothers and her sister, but not her. Of course, her dad wasn't affectionate toward any of them.

Being this close again with Dennis was hard on her, especially when he had given her promises and then broke them. JJ tried to pull away once more, this time he did loosen his hold, but didn't let her go.

"Talk to me, Jennifer Jean." Dennis said quietly. "Can we get back to where we were? We had good talks back then. Didn't we?"

JJ couldn't deny that remark, as those were the best conversations she had ever had with a guy. She looked up at him to give him a very brief nod. "Only if you tell me why?"

"Why, what JJ?" he asked with a puzzled voice.

"Why didn't you return my calls, answer my letters? Why did you break your promise to me?"

"What calls, what letters?" Dennis was at a complete loss now, he had thought she stopped contacting him because she found someone else to spend time with.

Now she tried harder to leave his embrace and walked to the coffee table to pick up her glass for a drink. "After you left for college, I tried every night to call you. Someone would answer and take my message for you. But not once did you call back. I wrote several times a week, never getting a reply back and after a couple months, got one back that said return to sender. I took that as your way to get rid of me."

Dennis never knew she had tried to contact him. The people in the dorm he was at had always been friendly enough to him, but he supposed there was someone there who was a prankster and kept his mail and messages from him.

"Jennifer Jean, I didn't know about your calls or letters. I gave you a promise and I have never knowingly broken a promise." He moved toward her again. "You have to believe me. I had never had anyone understand me the way you did and was a little surprised you didn't keep in touch."

She wanted to believe him; he was one of the few people in her life then who seemed to care about her too. "Why would someone hide your mail and messages?"

"I don't know, most of the guys on my floor were nice guys and I thought were friends. I can't say why someone did it, but I want you to know, you had been one of my best friends from home." Extending his hand, "Can we see past that and be friends again?"

JJ looked at his hand as a sign of forgiveness. She wanted, no needed, to believe him. Very cautiously, she placed her hand in his and for the first time noticed the difference in them.

The hesitation wasn't lost on Dennis. It was the first sign of trust, of accepting his friendship once again. Carefully, he closed his hand around hers. He, too, felt the difference immediately; his hard with some calluses, larger and stronger, hers was delicate and soft. With his eyes watching her, Dennis brought their joined hands to his lips and gently brushed her knuckles with a kiss.

Smiling at her, Dennis led her back toward the kitchen. He brought her over to the stools at the bar and pulled one out for her to sit. Then going in the galley, he opened the fridge, pulled out the open bottle of wine from the other night, found glasses and brought them to the bar. Dennis poured them each a glass before taking a stool next to Jennifer Jean.

"It's not your mom's snickerdoodles, but it will do." Tipping his glass toward hers, he clinked it with hers before taking a drink. "Now, are you still playing Roger's guitar?"

JJ couldn't help but laugh at the question as it was so far out of the normal line of thought for most men. "Yes," she took a sip of wine. "But I don't get to spend as much time with it as I had back then."

"How about your drawing? Do you still pick up a pencil and pad?"

She was embarrassed because he had remembered her one true passion, though she didn't know if he knew that. "No, not in a long time."

This shocked him, since she had talked about becoming a graphic designer. "Any particular reason why you stopped doing something that you loved so much?"

With a nonchalant shrug, "My priorities changed. What about you, no business for you?"

He liked this reacquaintance, with a chuckle he said, "No, during college I got introduced to extreme warrior sports, which lead to ROTC and recruiters then signing on to be in the Navy. From there, I went on to the SEALS. I met Thumper in basic and we have been friends and teammates ever since. We had a chance to opt out from the service a while back and now we do private security work for a former CO."

They talked, asking and answering questions, for nearly two hours, both realizing how much they had missed one another; it was like the years had slipped away, leaving them back at her quiet kitchen in the middle of the night. Dennis glanced at the clock hanging on the wall and couldn't believe how late it had gotten.

"I better go and let you get some sleep. I'll see you later."

For some reason JJ didn't want him to leave. "Dennis, would you mind," she stopped, reluctant to ask him to stay.

Carefully, he took her hand. "Would I mind what?"

Swallowing, then licking her lips, she started again. "Would you mind staying? I don't feel safe to be alone anymore."

Stunned by the simple request, Dennis smiled back at her. "Of course, I'll stay."

JJ shyly returned the smile. She got up and moved to the hall where she opened a door. "I'm sorry I don't have a spare bed, you'll have to sleep on the sofa." She took a couple of pillows and blanket off the shelf and turned to him.

"Don't apologize, the couch will be fine." Dennis took the bedding from her as she closed the linen closet door. Leaning over, he placed a friendly kiss on her forehead, "Go to bed, Jennifer Jean and sleep. I won't let anything happen to you tonight."

JJ looked up at him before turning and going to her room. "Good night Dennis." With that JJ entered her room, quietly closing the door.

Dennis put the bedding on the couch and looked around at her living room. He picked up all of their empty glasses, taking them to the dishwasher. He also took care of the other dirty dishes, wiped down the counters and table before going back into the living room. Dennis sent a quick text to Thumper about him staying at her request. Still too wired to sleep, he took the forgotten computer to the sofa, propped his feet on the coffee table and logged back on.

Quickly going into his email, he looked over the messages from Geek on JJ's new identity. Paul and Michaella had sent him the new info from JJ. It was all set and they would have the final documents in a day or two. He read messages from Gage, asking if they needed more help. He replied with a short note saying they had things currently under control, but would let him know if that changed.

He was about to log off when a new message arrived from Carrick. In it were new pictures of the baby Violet, Liam, Belinda and Carrick. He smiled and laughed out loud at them. He was filled with joy because Belinda was at last happy and had a family of her own. He sent a reply, hoping to see them all soon. He didn't elaborate on their quick departure and knew they wouldn't ask.

Quickly, Dennis brought up the screen telling him where Marco had been over the last twenty-four hours. He wasn't surprised to see that he didn't leave the restaurant right away. From there, he hit a local bar before going back to his hotel. JJ hadn't right out said anything about it, but Dennis got the feeling that she actually liked the guy. Time to dig into him and see if he could be used to help her out. He had limited access to law enforcement files, but from what was available to him, Marco hadn't ever been in any legal trouble. He shot a note to Geek for a deeper dig on the man. Dennis wanted to know whether to be wary or not about the man.

Chapter 12

When morning arrived, JJ wasn't ready for the day to start. She hadn't slept well even with Dennis in the other room. Their conversation the night before had brought up a lot of old feelings, ones she had thought she had buried.

Gradually, JJ got up and began her morning routine. Before she could leave the privacy of her own room, the aroma of fresh brewed coffee slipped into her room. With a smile, she walked out to see Dennis sitting at the bar with coffee and a bowl of cereal in front of him. He had a book open, propped open with another one. He looked up and smiled back at her.

"Good morning," he said. "I hope you don't mind, but being an early riser, I started coffee. I would have started breakfast too, but this was all I could find." The box of cereal hadn't been opened; JJ had bought it on impulse the last time she was in the store. At least it was fairly new and fresh.

JJ took the mug from the counter he set out to pour herself a cup. She went to the fridge and took out the flavored creamer and added it to her coffee. After taking a drink, she was amazed that the coffee tasted so good. He must have done something different to make such a great pot of coffee.

Looking at the titles of the books, she saw they were actually from her own shelf in the living room. With a twinkle in her eye she asked, "Couldn't sleep?" One book was a romance and the other a paranormal murder mystery.

He saw the amusement in her comment, "Just trying to broaden my horizons. Did you sleep well?"

With a shake of her head, "No, not really, haven't since he came 'into my life." She walked over and sat next to him. "Dennis, do you

67

really think I can run away from him and hide? Hide so he won't ever find me again?"

"Yes, honey. Geek has the expertise to build your new identity so no one will figure out who you were or where you are from. Thumper and I have the training in security and defense. We have contacts the average person doesn't have access to. Trust me. When you are ready, we will pack you up and leave this city behind and your father will have no clue where you are."

She really had no choice but to trust him at this point, there was no one else. JJ really didn't have friends; she had acquaintances but no one to really call a friend. If she would be honest with herself, Dennis and Michaella were the only friends she ever really had. Those months back when she was a teen were truthfully the best she could ever remember.

"Dennis, I am glad you are one of the people to help me." She was embarrassed to admit it, but it had to be said. "I have missed you, even though we really didn't know each other very long back then."

Not wanting her to feel more uncomfortable, he was reluctant to changed the subject. "JJ, I hadn't realized that I missed you too." Pushing the box toward her, he prodded her. "Are you going to have some breakfast?"

Not at all hungry, she shook her head no. Instead, JJ got up, and retrieved her own computer. After logging on, she went to her bank site and transferred more to the account Michaella had opened. Once that was done, she logged into that bank to check the balance before turning the screen toward Dennis.

"I asked Michaella to help me open this account about a year ago and I have been carefully adding funds to it ever since." She looked at Dennis. "I will move the last of my current bank funds to it once we have left and gotten out of the city. I can have Michaella then withdraw those funds and close the account." JJ took a drink of coffee. "Do you think this will be enough to live off for a while, at least until I can find a new way to make a living?"

Dennis was stunned, he looked at the balance in the account JJ had shown to him. Gads, how much did she make as a concierge? "I have no doubt, it will be enough. JJ, how the hell did you save nearly a half a million?"

She didn't hesitate, "I am very good at my job and my current employer knows how to compensate employees who excel in their job. Besides my salary, Mr. Turnquist has been generous with bonuses." She logged out and closed the laptop. "I get a break on my apartment rent since the building is owned by Turnquist's corporation and I don't spend money frivolously!"

"I didn't mean to imply anything negative by it." He had finished his cereal, so he got up taking his bowl to the sink to rinse before putting it in the dishwasher. He refilled his coffee cup and hers. Leaning back against the counter, he looked back to her. "I'll talk to Geek about finding a secure way to move all of your money to a protected account, so your father won't be able to use that as a means to find you or Michaella for that matter. We can't have that connection hanging over either of you."

He paused to gather his thoughts, "I will come to your office today as your mover to make arrangements. Pretend that it is our first meeting. I will lay out the process of the move, order boxes, and set a time frame."

He waited for a reaction from JJ, but not getting one continued, "Are you okay with this?"

JJ had to let it all sink in, she looked around her kitchen then turned to look at the living room she hardly spent time in. It just dawned on JJ that she wasn't as attached to this apartment as she had thought. It was a place for her to come to when she wasn't at work.

Turning back to Dennis, she slid off her stool, "I guess I am ready to leave." JJ glanced at the clock, "I'd better go or Marco will be knocking on the door. Did Michaella give you the key?"

"No, but I will call them and have them come and get me. We will lock up and head back to the hotel. I should be there around eleven, if that works for you?"

"Sure." JJ gathered her things, but stopped by the door, "Dennis, you don't think that Marco will recognize you from yesterday, do you?"

Dennis was puzzled, he hadn't realized she had seen him. "I hope not, but time will tell. If he was really good, he should question it, but let's hope he wasn't as observant as you." He took her hand, "How did you see me?"

"Ever since I had that first feeling of being watched, I have been more in tune with my surroundings, watching people that might be watching me. I saw both you and Paul yesterday."

Dennis might have to rethink having Thumper engage with Marco then. "Okay, I will see you later and we will talk more then."

Just then, there was the knock on the door and it startled both of them. JJ looked at the neat pile of bedding on the couch, then back to Dennis. He grabbed the stack and headed back toward the bedroom. All looked in place before JJ opened the door to find Marco there with flowers again. Instead of taking them back into the kitchen, JJ sniffed them and put them in the crook of her elbow as she closed and locked the door. Following the same motions of the past couple of days, they walked to the elevator, went down to the lobby and out to the waiting car.

As soon as the door was closed, Dennis came back out of the bedroom and walked to the window that overlooked the street. He watched as JJ came out, got in the car and Marco looked up and down the street, before getting in the car behind her. He dug his phone out and called Thumper; the sooner they came, the sooner he could get her away from Marco and safe.

At her office, JJ tried to concentrate on what work she had. She kept looking at the time on the computer screen, waiting for Dennis to arrive. He was prompt, knocking on her open door before stepping in. Introducing himself, he extended his hand toward her, before noticing the other man in the room. He turned to Marco and did the same toward him. Marco took the cue and left the office, but did not close the door. It only took JJ a moment to get up from her chair, cross the room and close the door herself. Dennis chuckled, and sat down across from her chair.

They carried on a casual conversation for several minutes. To make it look good, JJ called the maintenance man to her office and asked him to make a key for her apartment. He said it would only take a few minutes and he would be back shortly. As they waited, they shared more on their past. Henry came back with the key, a smile and left. After a few more minutes of talking, Dennis got up and left, but not before they had made plans for dinner for the evening.

Marco had to have been watching, because he came back in within seconds of Dennis departing. JJ didn't feel compelled to discuss the details with him, but he started asking her questions.

"So, were you able to set a day for them to start moving you?"

"Yes, it will be a few more days, maybe even next week. They are upgrading their trucks and will want one of them for my move. They also want to wait for an over the road driver to come back from paternity leave to make the move. He could use the money now that he has twins to support." The story rolled out of her mouth, almost naturally even though they hadn't even discussed it. She was a little surprised at it, hoping it didn't show on her face.

She tried to go back to her work, but apparently Marco wasn't satisfied. "JJ, I think I should check this company out, make sure they are the right company for your move."

Looking him directly in the eye, "You will do no such thing! I have used this company before, they are fast, competent and care for the items they are moving. I will not have you or anyone else doubting my decisions, not now and not in the future. Do you understand?"

He hadn't realized how powerful she actually was, and that he had just offended her. "I'm sorry JJ. I didn't mean to step out of line." A blush actually rose to his cheeks, "I will respect your decisions."

She gave him another look, one he had seen on her father's face, one that said she didn't want to be defied. When he finally looked away, she knew the subject was closed and went back to work. Until she actually left, she still felt responsible for the guests here at the hotel; past, current and future. She would miss this job; she knew for a fact.

At six that evening, JJ shut down her computer and gathered her things to leave for the day. Again, Marco tried to invite her out for dinner. She looked at him, and decided to really, really test the boundary of his loyalty to her father.

"Marco, I already have plans for the evening. Now, if you were to be really honest with me and tell me what you are hiding, I might, might change my mind and try to be friends with you."

She waited for him to give her what she was waiting for, but was only met with silence. It was telling and she would not offer any more to him either. The car pulled up in front of her building. Marco departed the car, looked around and held his hand for her, which she blatantly refused to take. The doorman opened the door, giving Marco a look. JJ walked to the elevator, not giving Marco another thought.

Once in her apartment, her thoughts changed to Dennis, Michaella and Paul. They had dinner made and waiting for her. Her smile was large and genuine. It was returned by all. Dennis came forward, took her things and escorted her to the table. He held her chair for her as she sat down. She almost missed that Paul had done the same for Michaella. They had a pleasant meal and light conversation.

"So, who do I have to thank for preparing such a fine meal?" JJ asked.

Paul, smiled and replied, "I was looking at some recipes on line and found these and wanted to try them. I hope you don't mind, me being in your kitchen?"

"Not at all," JJ said. "You can cook for me anytime." With that she turned to Dennis, "So do you cook too?" There was a twinkle in her eye, showing her complete amusement.

"Ah, not really." Dennis responded. "I can make most of the basics, like my mother had taught me, but I'll leave the difficult stuff for Thumper here!"

Her curiosity had finally gotten to her. "Okay, why do you call him Thumper?" She looked toward Paul and asked, "And why do you call him Spook?"

Both men looked at each other and returned her question with hearty laughter. When they were done, Dennis was the one to answer. Giving her the full story behind the nickname Paul sported. When he stopped, Paul picked up the story telling of the history behind Spook's nickname.

"Well, you see every team has to have someone to scout out a location or do recon. In our team, we hadn't really pinned it down to one person until it was Dennis's turn to give it a try. Apparently, he had been perfecting his stealth when no one was paying attention. He started by slipping into the barracks and pulling pranks on other members. Then he started to branch out into other team barracks, never getting caught. He got very proficient, of getting into and out of situations the rest of us couldn't. Spook got well known in the teams, so known, other CO's tried to have him transferred. Gage wouldn't have it though, wanting to keep our original team together."

Dennis looked at Paul, Michaella, then at JJ. "I have you to thank for my skills though."

Stunned, JJ said, "Me? Why?"

"Well, it drove me crazy how you were able to walk out of the kitchen, at night, in the dark and leave absolutely no trace to were you had gone. I didn't know how you did it and wanted to be just as good as that."

JJ laughed, "Really, it wasn't that hard. But I bet you never looked up."

"Up?" Dennis asked

"Up!" She said with a smile at the memory, "Mr. Willis, the neighbor behind us, had helped me finish the tree house my dad started for my brothers. They had lost interest in it and forgot it was there. When I found it, I fell in love and started to spend my time there. Mr. Willis was retired and needed to have something to do. We finished off the walls and roof, added electricity too." She stopped, in full recollection of a time and place that had really brought her joy. "Mrs. Willis even had a hand, donating house goods and food when they figured I wasn't getting enough at home."

Michaella reached over and took her hand in private support. Michaella had gotten a few details of her childhood, but hadn't realized it had been that bad.

"That first night then, when you were taking food from the house, you were going out and staying in the treehouse?" Dennis asked, appalled.

JJ just nodded.

Dennis had just gotten a new look at what she had actually gone through as a child. "Your family didn't know about the treehouse? Had they ever asked where you were going to?"

JJ couldn't look any of them in the eye, looking down at her hands folded in her lap just shook her head no.

Dennis got mad all over again at his old friend. After the week he spent with JJ's family and seeing how they had treated her, he pretty much ended his friendship with Roger. There was no way he could continue when he had seen how little Roger had cared for his sister, adopted or not.

"Jennifer Jean, why didn't you tell me?" Dennis asked gently, with real belated concern. "I would have done more, made sure you got more than food those nights." Now he was mad at himself.

JJ didn't know how to respond; the Willis's had become more than family to her. Dennis was the only other person beside Michaella to show her any concern.

She looked up then, "Don't Dennis, you had no idea and I couldn't say why I didn't feel up to sharing it. The treehouse became my refuge and Mr. and Mrs. Willis made sure that it was safe and warm. Mrs. Willis actually made better cookies than mom did, if you want to know the truth."

Now, Dennis laughed. "I guess I should be sorry that I didn't get to try them." He knew when to drop a subject, so went back to the nickname. "Anyway, the teams started to call me Spook, like a ghost, and it stuck. I got to enjoy the time out and alone, finding where my strengths in the woods were and expanding on them. Those skills still come in handy now and then."

The four turned the conversation to moving and getting JJ out of the city. Plans were made to bring in the boxes in three days and the truck in five. This would keep Marco from suspecting anything and her father thinking she was really moving out east.

Chapter 13

The days seemed to creep by. JJ spent her days at work, then her nights with Michaella, Paul and Dennis. Sometimes, it would be just Dennis and she looked forward to those more and more. Marco stopped asking to have dinner with her, for which she was grateful.

JJ had the meeting with Mr. Turnquist to request a leave for a family emergency. He wasn't happy but knew too the importance of family. He wouldn't say no to her, just wanted to be kept in the loop and updated on her return. It bothered her to lie to him, knowing she wouldn't be returning, but it just couldn't be helped either.

They had devised a plan for the boxes of the items that were to be going with her and those that would head east. Each box with items she wanted to keep would be marked with a white marker, all the rest were to be marked with a black marker for the room notation. Anyone watching from a distance shouldn't notice the difference, but yet they would be able to move them quickly into the second moving van.

Dennis and Paul had gone over the route several times, determining where the best place would be to switch the trucks. Then they had to consider Marco; he was the wild card. Since he had seen Paul at the restaurant, there was no way he could assist in the actual move; he would have to be the second van driver. They would call in a fellow team member to drive the truck out of the city.

JJ didn't have a lot of items to move and it looked like even less that she was going to keep. They had made the decision to start boxing this weekend, with them leaving the city mid to late week. Dennis could tell JJ wasn't happy to leave the career she loved, but also knew she didn't have a real choice if she was to get away from her father.

On the day for the packing to start, she dressed in jeans and a Tee, pulling her hair back. Since they had all been spending more time in her place, Michaella and Paul made sure the fridge was full and so she decided to make something for them to eat. Dennis had been spending full nights with her, giving her couch a lived-on feeling.

Dennis was pouring his second cup of coffee when JJ entered the kitchen. Her scent almost preceded her, he would recognize it anywhere. As a matter of fact, it was starting to drive his desire for her to a point where staying on the couch was getting hard to do. She brushed his hip as she passed by him and his body was on instant alert. He had started to see her as more than a friend; he was seeing her as a woman he desired.

"Good morning!" Dennis said, turning toward her and actually bringing her into his arms. The feeling of her in his embrace felt so natural; like they had done this for years, not for the first time.

She tensed at first, but then relaxed. "Good morning back!"

They stayed that way for several more heart beats before he released her. He had realized now that he had, he wished he hadn't. Having been with many women, he had never really allowed himself to get close to anyone; first because of his profession and second because maybe he was subconsciously looking for the one woman he could spend the rest of his life with, kind of like Thumper.

Thinking of his best friend, he had to smile again at the relationship Thumper had with Michaella. They literally ran into each other first in a liquor store, then met again at a coffee shop and the chemistry between them was instant and perfect. They had become a solid, permanent couple, who were already planning their wedding although they had only known each other for a few months. Timing apparently was everything.

Speaking of timing, they had better start with breakfast before the other two arrived, hungry and looking for something to carry them over until lunch time. They had a lot of sorting yet to do and the boxes to fill.

Clearing his throat, Dennis said, "Jennifer Jean, how about we get some breakfast rolling."

JJ glanced up at him with a different look on her face, a very lovely face, if he had to say so. He wasn't sure, but he thought perhaps she had felt the same thing he had while they were hugging. With one more look she took a step back, shook her head and moved over to the refridgeerator and started to pull eggs, bacon, English muffins and cheese from it to make breakfast sandwiches for them.

Almost forgetting about it, Dennis left the kitchen to go to his computer bag and dug through it until he found the pieces he was looking for. Going back to the kitchen, he asked JJ for her phone.

"Why?" she asked with a puzzled look, questioning his actions, but relinquishing it to him.

"Well," he started as he took the case and back off of it and removed the battery. "Since we know your father has been watching you, we want to make sure we could find you if we get separated." He wanted to be as honest as possible with her. "This is a tracking beacon." He showed her a very small item that resembled a piece of something that might actually be a part of the phone.

It was so small that it sat snuggly against some of the other circuits with in the phone. He tapped it with a small tool he also had. Then he turned the phone and shook it to make sure it didn't fall out on its own. Once he was positive it wouldn't come loose, he replaced the battery, snapped the back on and put the case back in place. He took his own phone out, tested the signal and then dialed her number. When it rang as it should he handed it back.

"Try to keep your phone always with you, this will work whether your phone is on or not. With the battery in or out." he said.

Taking a small velvet bag, he removed two more items. The first was the pendant, the second was a matching ring. Taking the necklace first, he came to her and looped it over her and fastened it around her neck. Then picking up the ring, Dennis took her right hand, which was unadorned. He slipped the ring on her third finger and was pleasantly surprised that it fit perfectly. They looked wonderfully natural on her, and no one would think they were anything more than two pieces of jewelry she had all of sudden decided to wear.

Snatching his phone up, he flipped to the app he had on his phone since Michaella had been taken by her ex.

"The necklace and ring are also tracking beacons. They are on slightly different frequencies from the phone, so they won't interfere with each other." He showed her the screen and it indicated three separate dots, each a different color. He explained how they work, the distance factor and how no one else would be able to detect them unless they knew the frequency they were on. Again, he stressed the importance to keep these two pieces on, even when she bathed or showered.

"Dennis, do you really think these are necessary? We know that it was Marco watching me and he has been staying close to me. Do you think my father would have someone else watching too?"

Taking both of her hands in his, Dennis looked down into her worried eyes. "JJ, Thumper and I learned a few months ago not to take anything for granted when we are dealing with someone we don't really know or trust. Michaella's ex kidnapped her right out of a busy store. Thumper was only several feet away. Her phone got dropped in the process and we wouldn't have had a way to find her if it weren't for the Fitbit she wears and the app on her phone. Luckily, Thumper knew her access code and our computer friend had been able to work a tracking algorithm into it."

He waited for her to acknowledge what he was saying before going on. "JJ, I am not taking that chance with you. With these pieces, we will always be able to find you, as long as you have one of them on you at all times. Okay?"

JJ looked at the seriousness in his face and knew he spoke the truth. She would trust he knew best and was doing this for her. She nodded her agreement. Within an instant, JJ was enveloped in strong arms and held against an even stronger chest.

Until that morning, he had been the perfect gentleman, but there had always seemed to be some unnamed chemistry between them and she wanted to explore it. Not here though, now was not the time.

Dennis looked into her eyes and then to her lips for only a brief second before he dipped his face to hers for a light kiss. It was the sweetest thing he had ever tasted. He wanted more but kept it simple and light. When her eyes opened, he was smiling at her. She, too, had felt that instant connection.

Before any words could be said by either of them, there was a knock at the door. In unison, they both looked at the door and laughed. Dennis released her and went to open the door, while she took a pan out of the cupboard to start the breakfast sandwiches.

Paul joined her, first giving her a friendly hug before rolling up his sleeves and helping her with the easy meal she was preparing. He always seemed to be the first one in the kitchen; he liked to cook and wasn't afraid to show it.

They laughed through the meal prep, which they ate around the kitchen bar instead of using the table. The clean-up was almost joyous. Actually, the whole day seemed joyous; JJ didn't dwell on the leaving, but of a new start. After today, she was actually looking forward; forward to the new beginning her mother had actually intended.

Chapter 14

As the moon rose, long after Michaella and Paul left, Dennis came to her with two glasses of wine as she sat on the floor, going through her books. Handing one to her, he joined her on the floor, but stretched out his long legs and leaned back on one elbow, looking at her. It almost unnerved her with his intense gaze.

Finally, she couldn't take it anymore. "What?" JJ asked.

"Nothing," he said casually. Taking a drink of his wine, he inquired, "Has anyone ever told you how beautiful you are?"

Stunned, she just gaped at him. He could see that perhaps no one had. "Really JJ, you are!"

Leaning over, he kissed her lips. Just a soft brushing at first. He felt her intake of a breath more than he heard it. Now, he leaned back to looked at her, a smile of satisfaction spreading across his own face. She was so sweet tasting, he had to have another sample of it.

JJ took a quick sip of her wine before he could kiss her again. It surprised her when her glass was taken from her hand and set aside. Dennis took the hand that was holding the glass and nibbled gently on her cold fingers, constantly watching for her reaction.

Slowly, her hand warmed; so, did her arm, shoulder and the rest of her. She hadn't known the hand could be so responsive to a man's lips or teeth and the responses would go farther up her arm. Just when she accepted his kisses, he nipped at the pad at the base of her thumb. A shiver ran through her whole body!

Dennis felt her reaction, which pleased him. It meant she wasn't immune to him like she had probably been with other men. It was then that a thought came to him: had she ever been with a man? He didn't think so but was going to find out.

Carefully he asked, "JJ, have you had any long-term boyfriends?"

Shyly, she shook her head no.

"Have you had a short-term one?"

Again, the shake of the head.

Stunned he couldn't let it go and it was his turn to be puzzled. "Why the hell not?" He cooled his temper. "Sorry, the guys around you must have been complete asses!"

Her eyes widened. JJ swallowed, took a breath and said, "Actually, after the first or second date, I wouldn't hear from them. Come to find out from Marco, my father was seeing to it that none of the boys I dated got more than one or two dates. He had them all scared off."

Now Dennis really hated her father and was getting close to some unknown emotion toward this Marco. "He told you that? Did he say why?"

Reaching for her glass, JJ took a fortifying drink before she went on. "When he told me, I asked why too? Marco said that my father wanted to make sure that I stay a virgin. So, he must have some kind of plan, or someone he wants to marry me off to." Drinking again, she pondered that herself. "Do you really suppose that is why, all of a sudden, it is so important that I'm in New York?"

Was she going to be leverage in some deal? She hadn't spent any time in thinking about it, but with what she knew about the man called her father, he probably didn't do anything unless he benefitted from it. It would always have to be a win for him and loss for the other guy.

Dennis could see the wheels turning in that pretty little head and didn't doubt her words for a minute. As a kingpin in a family that was into all kinds of illegal activities, he also didn't doubt Giovanni would use his own daughter to his advantage in a business deal. Fortunately, they would be the ones to win this time and he would lose. He made a mental list to call a few contacts and get a little more info on his recent activity, his associates and even enemies. It was always better to be prepared for all contingencies.

"Don't worry about it! We will make sure you are way out of his reach." Dennis said, again taking the wine glass away.

Gently, he tugged her hand, having her tumble to the floor. JJ lay on her back looking up at him. He almost thought she looked vulnerable, but there was something else in her eyes now. They had taken on an intent expression. One saying she had forgotten their previous discussion and had moved on to the intimacy of their positions.

Reaching forward, Dennis pulled her closer, almost beneath him. Now they were leg to leg, hip to hip and chest to chest. His features had also changed; his pale eyes were now more determined. This time, he was going to taste more of her, get to know that taste and for her to know his. Leaning forward his lips touched hers, tentative at first then with more intent. Sweeping his tongue over her lips, Dennis slipped it into her generous mouth. JJ released a small gasp of wonder, before acceptance, then hunger.

Without another thought, Dennis took what JJ was giving him: trust. Their tongues danced together, hers hesitant at first, then learning and forging ahead, full steam. JJ went from novice to experienced in the quickened beats of their hearts. His blood heated so fast, Dennis had to slow this down. There was nothing he wanted more than to strip her bare and have her right there on the floor. Her inexperience, her virginity, though was a really good reason to slow this down. He had to be the one to make that decision.

Breaking the kiss, Dennis eased up, nibbling at her now swollen lips. They were both breathing hard, hearts hammering away. Reluctantly, he eased up enough to look down at her. She slowly opened her eyes and gazed up at him. He had never seen anyone more beautiful than JJ at that moment. His own heart did a little triple beat. Smiling at her, he knew he should say something.

"Wow!" Dennis said in a low, breathless voice. He rested his forehead against JJ's as he tried to gather his thoughts. "JJ," he started, "You have to know how much I want to continue this, but is now the right time and is this the right place?"

JJ realized he was giving her a choice to continue or to stop. It was all up to her and for once she wasn't completely sure of herself. In the past, the choice had always been taken out of her hands by the guy. Now, with Dennis, she had the opportunity to go beyond a few kisses, but was she really ready to start this with him when her future was so up in the air? She guessed there was no better time than now to ask.

"Dennis, I want to be with you too, but," she trailed off, closing her eyes and turning her head slightly away from him.

"But what, honey?" Gently, he turned her face back to look at him. "Talk to me JJ."

It took her several seconds of looking into his amazing eyes before she continued. "What happens tomorrow? What happens if we don't get away?" What happens if we do? Where will I be going and what will I be doing?"

Now he could really see the tormented place she really was at. She was completely right in asking all of these questions and so many more. All he could do was reassure her the best he could.

"JJ, we are going to get you away, and you have enough money set aside to take the time to decide what you want to do and where you want to go. For now, let's just plan on you coming back to the little community where Thumper and I have places. Michaella will be moving in with him and I am sure you could stay at her house until you have made more firm plans. Okay?"

Seeing the thoughtfulness and sincerity in his eyes, JJ nodded her agreement.

Giving her another light kiss, Dennis rolled over and smoothly got to his feet and offered a hand to her. Effortlessly, he lifted her up once she had given him her hand. Once they were on their feet, he brought her toward his hard body. She went willingly until there was barely any space between them. Putting her arms around him, she closed the gap, resting her head on his chest.

They simultaneously released a comforting sigh. Standing with him, breathing in his scent, was like coming home. She had never realized that a person, not a place, could make her feel so good. She felt safe within his arms too. Feeling safer than she had felt in since this whole bizarre thing had started, when she felt she was being watched.

It was getting late and they needed to get some sleep. Dennis pulled away just enough to look down at the woman in his arms. "It's getting late, we should the hit the rack."

She nodded her agreement but was reluctant to let him go. For years she was able to be alone and was comfortable. Now with Dennis here, and the threat she sensed coming at her, she wasn't sure she wanted to be alone.

"Dennis, I want to ask something." JJ started, really apprehensive about what she was doing.

"Ask away." He said casually.

Not sure if she was ready for this, JJ said, "Forget it, it was nothing." She turned to walk away to her room.

Stopping her with a light touch on her arm, Dennis said, "JJ, it's okay. Just talk to me. Ask me?"

Swallowing slowly, she looked up at him still unsure, "Dennis, would you lay with me, just until I fall asleep?"

Now, she had stunned him, he hadn't expected her to ask that. "JJ." He paused, her light tremors made it easy for him to respond. "JJ, go get ready for bed and I will join you shortly."

Bobbing her agreement, she skirted around the boxes in the spare bedroom and headed to her own room, where the boxes were also starting to stack up. Pulling out her nightwear, she quickly slipped out of her day clothes and changed. Stepping into the bathroom, she washed her face, smeared on her night cream and quickly brushed her teeth. She was sliding into bed when there was a light knock on the door.

Answering, JJ settled into bed. Dennis turned off the light, removed his shoes, jeans and tee shirt. He slid into the bed, pulling JJ against him in a comfy spooning position. He heard her sigh and noticed she was no longer trembling.

After a few minutes, she broke the silence with a quiet question. "Dennis, what were you doing out there?"

Nestling her closer, he answered with an almost sleepy tone how he cleaned up the dishes, checked the doors, did a quick check of his email and messages, sent replies and finished off with counting loaded boxes.

The last items had her giggling silently next to him. "Good night Dennis." After a thought, she added, "Thank you!" With that, JJ took a deep breath, exhaled and nodded off to sleep.

Dennis was pretty sure she didn't even hear him say, "You're welcome, JJ."

He smiled into her hair, taking in its unique scent. He lay there a long time trying to determine exactly what it was. He then caught a whiff of her skin. It had the same essence! He smiled to himself and settled in and closed his own eyes. He wasn't sure he would go to sleep, but he drifted off as quickly as she had.

Chapter 15

As they had planned, the truck was backed up to the back of the building. JJ stood there looking at it apprehensively, half filled with furniture and boxes. It was clearly evident now that she was leaving the life she had come to love. The city, her career, her work associates, everything here meant the world to her because she had done everything to make this her life as she wanted it to be. In her head, she knew she needed to get away and hide from her father. In her heart, she was very sad to cut this part of her life short.

Dennis saw JJ standing there when he came down with some of the last boxes. She had a pale, faraway look, that almost seemed as if she was unsure about what they were about to do. Setting his boxes down, he went and gathered her into his arms. He wasn't worried about anyone, especially Marco, seeing them. Being in the back of the building, there was actually a protective overhang to shield tenants as they brought in their belongings into or out of the apartments.

Marco had told JJ he would come to help load the truck after he finished up some errands, saying he would be booking airline tickets for JJ and himself. She hadn't told him how she had planned on making it a road trip with Michaella, and Dennis smiled at the money he would lose by assuming she would fly with him. The man just wasn't smart enough to get over the crush he had on the woman he had been stalking for the last few years. Dennis almost pitied him! Marco's vision was so tainted, he couldn't see how he was being used, first by his boss and second by the woman he was to protect.

Dennis didn't blame the guy; JJ was an amazing woman and he intended to keep her. The only regret he had was not staying in touch with her all these years. Well, he couldn't turn back time, just make sure that he didn't make the same mistake twice.

When Michaella and Thumper came down with more boxes, JJ stepped away from Dennis looking up at him with wide eyes. He wondered what was going through her mind at the moment. Since they had been sleeping together, but not being intimate, her whole demeanor had changed. She had told him that she hadn't slept as well in a very long time. Having him with her at night, eased something within her, easing her mind and making her feel safe, so she could sleep. He smiled to himself, knowing he could do that for her.

When the last box was in the truck and the door brought down and locked, JJ turned and saw Marco standing off to the side. She couldn't read the expression on his face or in his eyes. A quick look toward Dennis, told her all she needed to know at this time. Dennis was here for her and always would be. Marco was here for her father, a job, not for her personally.

Marco stepped up to her, "JJ, I have the car waiting to take us to the airport." He moved to take her elbow to escort her to the front of the building.

JJ jerked her arm away, "No, I'm riding with Michaella. We've decided to drive, talk and have some girl time."

Marco saw the defiance and really couldn't blame her, but her father was pretty clear that he wanted her in his house by nightfall.

"JJ, please you must come with me. Your father had made plans for this evening after I told him we would be there today."

Dennis could see it coming and he smiled at her before he turned.

"Mighty presumptuous of you, don't you think?" JJ took a breath before going on. "As I told you before, I will not be told what to do, not by you and certainly not by him. We have already made reservations along the way, and I'm keeping every one of them."

"JJ," He started, saw the determination in her decision and the way she was standing, hands fisted on her hips. "Please, don't anger him, come with me!"

"NO!"

Taking the keys from her pocket, she said, "I'll just run the keys up and take one last look around the apartment." It was in her tone, she wanted a few minutes alone, so all of them stayed on the loading dock. With that, JJ turned and swiftly climbed the first set of stairs before an arm reached out and grabbed her and a cloth was clapped across her face and the world went dark.

Marco pulled his phone out and moved away from them to make a call after JJ went back into the building. Dennis watched him and the reaction he got as he talked to the person on the other end of the phone. It didn't take much to see who he was speaking with: his boss. You could actually see him cringe away and the man was hundreds of miles away. He disconnected the call and stuck the phone back into his breast pocket.

"JJ went upstairs minutes ago. She should have been back down by now." Marco said as he rejoined them.

Dennis had an itchy feeling running up his spine! He kept looking toward the door when Thumper came over. Glancing over at Marco, he asked the question without opening his mouth.

Dennis started toward the door, before Thumper stopped him by stepping in front of Spook.

"Let's give her a minute or two more, Spook. Marco is here, she'll be fine."

Dennis's gut was telling him something wasn't right and when Marco made the move toward the door, Spook beat him to it and ran up the stairs. They found her purse on the first landing, spilled with all of her things spread around like there had been a struggle. Since they were at the back door, it meant she must still be in the building or might have been taken out the front, which didn't make any sense as it would have raised suspicion. Thumper raced to the front entrance and saw nothing out of place. So, where the hell was she? It only took a second for Spook to turn on Marco.

With speed, training and experience, Spook had the other man up against the wall with both hands gripping the other man by this expensive suit lapels. His face was only a fraction of an inch away as he spit out rapid-fire questions.

Thumper had returned from the front, to pull his friend off the other man. Marco was clearly out of his element, against two men trained in combat. All he could do was try and protect himself.

"I don't know!" Marco yelled as he shoved Thumper and tried to move toward the steps. Thumper grabbed him again and held on. "Get off me!"

"Marco, just tell us where she is and we'll let you go."

"I just told you, I don't know where she is." Marco looked between the two men and for the first time, really saw them. These men were more than movers. He saw pure determination to protect JJ. "I'm telling you the truth, I don't know. I wouldn't do anything to hurt her."

"Really," Spook started, "You knew more than you were telling her. She knew it and so do we. If you really wanted to help her, you would have told her." Spook clenched his fists, fists that wanted action.

Thumper used his strength now to push the slightly smaller man against the wall. "Who else knew she was here and leaving today, other than her father?"

"Just me." Marco was looking between the two men who still had him against the wall, caged in and angry. He had always been able to handle himself in a fight, but in this instance, he knew he wouldn't come out on top. Just knowing it, worried him.

Spook moved in closer, with a quiet, contained voice said, "What did her father have planned for her, once she got to New York?"

Knowing he didn't have a choice, he answered. "Giovanni was

going to give her to a rival as a part of a deal to add to his smuggling business. Watters is an animal! He uses women and not nicely either, he is brutal and vicious."

This steamed Spook. "You knew this and were just going to stand by and let it happen. I thought you had feelings for her?"

Marco turned green at that point. Ashamed of himself he dropped his head, couldn't look either of these men in the eye.

As much as Spook wanted to beat the living tar out of Marco, he stepped back, looked at the ceiling and tried to bring his anger back into check.

"Thank God I took precautions against something like this happening." He walked over, picked up her purse, and pawed through it until he found her phone, which was easy as the rest of her belongings were all over the floor and the cell was tucked in its special pocket. "Fuck!" He looked over at Thumper.

"You put a beacon in her phone." It really wasn't a question.

Taking his own phone out of his pocket, he brought up the program to locate the other beacons. As he had suspected, it showed the phone beacon right where they stood, but the other two were moving away from their location.

Without a word, he started toward the door and saw Michaella standing there as pale as a ghost. He had been so focused on JJ, he had forgotten about Michaella.

"Michaella," he started, walking over to her, "Someone grabbed JJ. We'll find her. We have to!"

Michaella took one look at his determined face and knew there was more between the two. She had suspected it over the last few days, but hadn't said anything. Then she remembered what had happened to her only a short time ago and couldn't believe that it was happening again. She also knew if anyone could find her, it would be Dennis and Paul.

"Just make sure you do!" She stepped aside and let him pass as

Paul came to her. He didn't have to say anything to her. They had developed a unique way of communicating just by being together.

Out on the loading dock, Dennis glanced at his phone to get a sense of the direction she was being taken. They were taking her east; no surprise there. He raced to his truck and was closing his door when Thumper got in the passenger side.

"Let's go get her buddy!" Thumper looked back over his shoulder and gave Michaella a deep, telling look. "Move Spook, before we lose her."

Dennis didn't need to be told twice. The engine roared to life and they were headed in the direction of the beacon. He was glad he had decided on more than just one; if he had only put one in her phone, they would haven't been able to track her.

They continued to move away from the city, through business districts, then high end residential to the seedier parts of the big city to industrial. Where in the hell were they going, he wondered?

After following for forty minutes, they still didn't seem to be getting any closer. Dennis pushed his speed knowing if he was stopped by a local cop, they would lose JJ. He had to risk it, there was no way he would lose her again.

Noticing all of a sudden that her beacons stopped, Dennis looked around the desolate area. What could they mean by bringing her here? Then they heard it, the undeniable whap, whap, whap of a helicopter. Panic went through both of them, because there would be no way to track her if she was put on the helicopter and flown away.

Getting to the edge of the empty lot, Dennis stopped when he saw the two cars and seven men getting out of them, but no sign of JJ. Seven against two, not good odds, even if the two were trained SEALS. They hadn't prepared for this; if the seven hadn't had guns, there was no way to take them and ensure JJ wasn't hurt.

Swearing a sailor's blue streak, he called the only person that could help them now, Gage. Their former commanding officer still had the connections to get them the help they would need now.

"Gage, does your offer for help still stand?" Dennis didn't even take the time for the usual pleasantries.

"Spook, that you? This better be damned important!" It sounded like Dennis interrupted something, looking at the clock in the dash and calculating the time difference. Gage and Marlena may still be in bed, and not sleeping.

"It is Gage! Remember the person Thumper and I left there to help?"

Dennis stopped, watching as a limp JJ was taken from one car and hefted into the helicopter. He could see she was bound and blindfolded, but wasn't moving. Thumper had retrieved the binoculars to get the call numbers from the chopper before it left the ground.

"Spook, talk to me! Tell me what the hell is going on?"

"Fuck Gage, they just loaded JJ into a helicopter and we can only guess at this point as to where they are taking her."

"Tell me what you need, I'll get on the phone, then I'll head that way."

Gage listened as Dennis gave him a brief run down on JJ, her biological father and the man they suspected to have abducted her. Thumper was on the phone already to Geek to see if he could work on tracking JJ's remaining two beacons.

Dennis grabbed the paper with the number from the helicopter, recited them to Gage and listened as Gage laid out his thoughts and the direction he was thinking in ways of finding JJ. He told Spook to give him an hour and he would be back with him with more information. At that point, Gage hung up and Dennis was looking at his dead phone. All they could do at this point was wait. They turned around and headed back to where Michaella waited for word about her friend.

Chapter 16

When they got back to JJ's apartment building, they found Michaella and Marco were still there, sitting in Michaella's car. The car Marco had come in was gone. They both got out as they saw Dennis's truck pull up.

Going against all of his need to pummel Marco, Dennis walked up to the man and roughly shoved him in the back of his truck. Thumper had helped Michaella into her car and waited for Dennis to pull out in front of them. They would go back to their hotel and wait for Gage to call them back. While they were doing that, Dennis would get more information out of Marco, one way or another.

Going into their rooms, hauling in Marco with him, Dennis started drilling Marco. Had he called anyone? Who has he been in contact with? Who else knew about JJ, other than her father? Who might have taken her? Where might they take JJ? Would they hurt her? Why would they take her if her father was going to give her over anyway? Solemnly, Marco answered each and every question, holding nothing back.

Dennis was surprised when Marco said he hadn't called his employer, JJ's father, again.

"So why wouldn't you call him?" he probed. "Aren't you afraid of what he might do when he finds out?"

Marco just gave a shrug, Giovanni was going to give her to that animal and there was really nothing he could do about it, he had thought. He refused to tell JJ, and now knew she had been asking for his help and he hadn't given that to her. At this point, he didn't care what happened to him as long as he could help get her back, unharmed.

"I'd been following her so long, falling in love with the person she seemed to be, that I guess I couldn't see anything else." Marco stood and moved away from the other man's reach. "I want to help now." He had learned from Michaella while they waited about their plan to hide JJ. "Tell me what I can do to help get her back. I will make sure that your plans can continue, and you get her away from her father."

The change in Marco wasn't hard to see. They had to trust him enough to keep his word; he really didn't have anything to lose. Dennis knew his feelings for JJ had changed; he knew it was simple for a man to fall in love with her. JJ wasn't there to look for more than what she expected from herself. In doing that, she accomplished what others wanted, gaining their approval and respect.

"Tell us everything you know about the animal her father was going to trade her to. Don't leaving anything out. We know what kind of criminal her father already is and will deal with that later." Thumper said.

Spook was working really hard at holding on to his control. He was trying to work a plan to get her back when his phone rang.

"Hey, Gage what do you have?" he asked desperately. He put the speaker on so they all could hear the conversation. He looked at Marco, starting the fine line to trust him.

"I was able to contact someone out east in the judicial system and they have been working on getting Giovanni locked up for years. There is actually a special task force who has been working at trying to get someone inside of his organization. Unfortunately, every time they do, he finds out and the agent is found dead. There are two brothers working through the DEA and FBI that have managed to get more information on Giovanni and also Watters. I emailed their information to you so you can contact them for more assistance."

Gage stopped and they heard some mumbling in the background before he came back on the line.

"Spook, our best shot at this point is to work with the Lattimer brothers. Get them the frequencies of the beacons and let's see what they can find out. I am heading to the airport now. Henry is firing up the jet and we will be in Chicago in a few hours. Have you heard from Geek?"

Thumper responded, "Yea, he is working on the beacons, but since they are in the air, it was going to be hard for him to find them until they land. Once on the ground, he was sure it wouldn't take him long to locate her." He took Michaella's hand. "We are pretty sure they are headed back to New York, so that was where he was going to concentrate his search."

Marco listened and realized that he might have found a way out of the crime family he hadn't realized that he hated. These men could help him with that, if they would trust him that was. He would wait until the call was done, see what was being decided and help where he could.

After more talking, it was decided that they would all travel to New York, only having Henry stopping long enough to refuel and the three of them to get on the jet. Gage finally said his good-byes and disconnected the phone. Spook got up and paced the small room. Thinking, pondering and analyzing the situation, trying to work it all through in his head before saying anything out loud. He stared at his phone, looking at the info Gage had emailed on the task force. The message was short and to the point. The Lattimers had a military background before going to work for the alphabet agencies.

He sent a text to Geek, asking for more background info on the brothers. He would want to see what their qualifications were first, then how best to use what they were good at. While he waited for the info, he worried about JJ. Clearly, she had been drugged, but had they done anything more to her. He hoped to hell they hadn't. It didn't really matter since they would pay for abducting her in the first place, positively starting with her father.

Grabbing a bottle of water, Dennis was twisting off the top when the email came back from Geek. Seems the Lattimer brothers had been army, and snipers at that, then to specials operations. Both were well respected with handfuls of commendations. They had then been recruited by the alphabet soup gangs, as most military thought of the FBI, CIA, DEA and other various agencies. Again, with commendations and highly earned respect.

Dennis handed his phone to Thumper to confirm his own thoughts. A raised eyebrow and a grunt that most wouldn't understand, Thumper gave the phone back and Dennis used it to call the number he had been given. It was answered on the second ring so Gage must have paved the way with a call or his contact made a call.

The conversation hadn't lasted more than fifteen minutes. In that time, they had a location to meet the brothers in New York who would provide them with accommodations so no one would need hotel rooms. When he disconnected, Dennis turned once again to Marco.

"Alright Marco, time to see if you really are telling the truth and are willing to help."

Marco looked at Dennis with his ghost like eyes then to the other big man and then to Michaella. He could see now how the men had gotten their respective nicknames: Spook and Thumper. Spook with the pale eyes and Thumper the pure physical size and strength. "I'll help you any way I can, but I want out too. I just realized that I had stayed only because of JJ. I can't justify it anymore."

Hearing that, Dennis was going to take full advantage of it. "We will be able to get into the city, the Lattimers will have a car for us, but we really need to know what to expect from Giovanni and this Watters."

Looking toward Thumper to get reassurances, he went on, "How many men does this Watters have and where would we expect to find him?"

They talked and strategized until it was time for them to meet Gage at the small airstrip. They took their few belongings and headed out to the truck.

Chapter 17

JJ slowly came to, with a headache and rolling stomach. Her arms tingled and her shoulders yelled as pain rolled through them. She didn't open her eyes, just listened to judge her surroundings. She could hear men talking and a television playing. JJ didn't want them to know she was awake. She was smart enough to learn what she could, without them knowing they were giving out information.

She wondered if the men worked with her father or someone else. As she listened, JJ heard the talk of an ambush against some of her father's men. She almost smiled! Good for them, hit him hard. It was then she wondered why she had been taken.

Very carefully, JJ used her thumb to check and see if the ring Dennis gave her was still in place. She almost sighed her relief out loud because it was still on her finger. Not risking to check for the necklace, JJ assessed her condition. Other than the headache and upset stomach which seemed to be settling, she thought she was okay. Her hands were bound behind her back but they hadn't bothered with her feet.

Opening only one eye, she looked around the room carefully. There were two men seated on a couch with their backs to her, watching a football game on the television that was mounted on the wall above an unlit fireplace. They were the only ones besides herself in the room. She opened the other eye and saw she was on a bed in a room separated by open French doors. Behind her on the right was the bathroom and the left, a closet. She could see only part of the room on the other side of the open doors. She wasn't sure if she was in an apartment or hotel suite.

Looking toward the window and the darkening sky, told her that it must be early evening. Not knowing how long she had been unconscious, JJ knew by the outside light it had been hours since she had left her apartment. How long would it take Dennis to find her? Then she wondered if she was even still in Chicago?

Just then, one of the men stood; she closed one eye but watched him walk to the left side of the room before returning with two beers. Handing one to the other man, he set his down and stalked to the right side where a door stood slightly open. He entered and closed the door. Bathroom she thought. After a couple minutes he came back out and sat back down, taking a swig of his beer.

JJ thought it odd that he hadn't come to check on her. He must have thought whatever they drugged her with would last longer. She would try to take advantage of the fact that they didn't know she was alert. Testing the bed's springs, she carefully rolled on to her back. It made no sound, which was good for her. Slowly, JJ rolled to the edge of the bed and dropped her legs over the side and sat, waiting to see if her captors noticed.

When they made no movement toward her, she stood. Her head swam and her vision blurred to the point that she had to sit back down. Quickly, she looked out to the other room again. Still no movement. Waiting until her vision cleared, she continued to sit on the side of the bed.

JJ pulled on the restraints on her hands. They weren't too tight and seemed to be of cloth not rope. She wondered if she could do like they did in the movies and twist enough to get her arms back around to the front of her body. She found out she wasn't as limber as she used to be and her efforts were useless.

As she sat thinking, she realized she needed to go to the bathroom and something to drink might be nice. There was no way she could use a restroom trussed like the Thanksgiving goose, so she would have to ask the men to let her loose long enough to relieve herself and get some water. She would have to get their attention and see just what kind of men they were.

Taking a calming breath, JJ cleared her throat. When neither of the men moved, she became more vocal.

"Excuse me," she said. Turning toward the men, she tried to stand then dropped to her knees, pretending to be too weak to stand. Maybe if they thought she was helpless, they wouldn't be as concerned if they freed her hands.

The man who had gotten up to the beers earlier stood and came toward her. The other man turned his head to look at them but then the TV drew his attention again.

"Could I get a drink of water and use the restroom, please?" JJ still tried to come off as weak and submissive. She had learned from her self-defense instructor to make the aggressor think you were weak and attack when they least expected it.

Looking down at her as he towered above, he nodded then reached behind and untied her hands. "Use the bathroom, then I will have water for you when you come out. Don't try anything stupid! We aren't supposed to hurt you, but all bets are off if you get anything in that pretty head of yours."

Wobbly, JJ got to her feet, grabbing his arm like she was unsteady. He actually helped her to the door of the bathroom before turning to back into the other room. JJ closed the door, and quietly locked it before searching the room for anything that might be used as a weapon. Like a typical hotel bathroom, there were the little bars of soap, shampoo, lotions and towels. Unlike a hotel though, this bathroom had a vanity with actual drawers for putting personal items in. She used the toilet, ran water to wash her hands and face while quietly pulling each of the drawers open and inspecting them.

It was in the bottom one where she found the old razor blade wedged in the back slightly under the side. Thank heaven for poor construction, or she would never have found it. JJ took the blade and wrapped it in toilet paper before stuffing it into her jean pocket. Then drying her hands, she turned off the water and opened the door.

Sitting on the night stand was a bottle of water, a candy bar and a wrapped sandwich. Sitting down next to the items, she took the water, opened it and took a healthy drink. Capping it, JJ picked up the sandwich and turned it over in her hands, trying to decide exactly what kind it was.

"It's ham and cheese. I didn't know what kind you might like, so picked the most common."

"Thank you," JJ said as she set it back down. "Maybe later, my stomach is a little queasy."

She looked up at him, wondering how much information she could get out of him. "Where am I?"

"You don't need to know that." Turning, he started to back into the other room.

"Wait," when he turned back, she asked, "What is your name?"

"You don't need to know that either!"

At his back, she said quietly, "Please?" She was sure he wouldn't answer, but then heard him say Woody. Watching him go back to the couch and sit down almost relieved her. Taking the water again, she drank some more before going to the window. Carefully, she opened the drape just enough to see they were about ten floors up in an impressive hotel. The area below was busy with foot and auto traffic, so they were in a pretty large city. Since she didn't see any landmarks that she recognized in the dark to be Chicago, they had taken her somewhere else.

Letting the drapes close, JJ went back to the bed, pulled the covers down and crawled in. There was no way that she would allow herself to sleep though, she didn't trust the men in the other room to leave her alone. Woody said that she wasn't to be harmed, but she wouldn't put it past them to try and force themselves on her and rape her.

Chapter 18

Dennis was going crazy waiting for Gage to get there. He wanted to be out searching for JJ, although, he knew also they needed more information as to where she might be. The Lattimers were able to find a general location, within about a five-block area in New York. That still left a lot of terrain to cover without pinpointing it down more. He was sure if he could get his feet on the ground there, his instincts would kick in, along with his phone app, and he would be able to find her.

He was pretty sure the kidnappers had something special in mind for her, otherwise why take her in the first place. What they needed was to figure out what that might be and get to her before anything bad would happen to her. He was glad he had put inconspicuous beacons on her and they were working.

Dennis got up and started pacing the room again. Stopping in front of Marco, he balled his fists and walked back to the window. More than he had ever wanted anything, he wanted to pound the life from Marco, a man who had claimed he would never hurt JJ. How could he have worked for a man who would use his daughter as a pawn in a deal to gain him more in wealth and status? Shaking his head, Dennis turned and was about to say something to Marco when his phone went off.

"Hello," listening, he kept his eyes on Marco. "We're on our way." He slid the phone in his pocket, "Gage will be landing in about twenty minutes," and looking at Thumper said, "Grab what you need and we will meet him at the airstrip."

Thumper and Michaella exchanged looks and moved quickly toward the door. Marco stood, but didn't move beyond that.

"I want to go with! I can help find her. I know Giovanni and his organization. I will be able to get information for you."

Dennis had really considered leaving him here, until Thumper gave him a silent look that told him otherwise.

"You can go! But if you screw this up, I will drop you where you stand and not give another thought about it. Understand?"

Marco glanced at Thumper then back to Spook. He was getting a better appreciation for their nicknames by the minute. He only nodded before moving toward the door.

A slap on the back from Thumper gave Spook only a slight reassurance that he was doing the right thing. In the parking lot, Thumper grabbed a black duffel from the trunk of Michaella's car along with her flowered bag. Taking them both, he flipped the tailgate of Spook's truck open, tossed them in before opening the back door for Michaella. He eyed Marco before getting in the shotgun seat. Marco walked around to the rear driver side door and got in before Spook could change his mind.

Henry was just touching down when they pulled into the airstrip. Waiting for the plane to stop they stood by the side of the truck with their bags sitting on the tarmac. Marco was several paces away, waiting for them to decide he wasn't welcome to come. The jet passenger door opened, the stairs dropped and Gage stuck his head out.

"You ready?" Gage called.

That was all it took for Spook, Thumper and Michaella to move toward the plane. Gage stepped out and helped Michaella up into the plane. Spook stopped short of entering and looked back at Marco.

"Are you coming?" Spook asked.

Marco didn't wait, but jogged over to the plane.

Spook did a quick introduction, "Gage this is Marco, the jerk who has been watching JJ for years, knowing her criminal father was going to hand her over to an animal in a deal to further his illegal operation." With that said Spook got into the plane.

Gage stuck his hand out, "Gage, nice to meet you Marco. Let's talk on the plane, because if we don't get on right away, Spook will have Henry take off without us."

They got on the plane; Gage pulled the stairs and closed the door, then told Henry to call the tower for clearance to leave.

Marco looked into the cabin, seeing Thumper and Michaella sitting next to each other. Spook was across the aisle. There was another man slumped in a seat behind Spook sound asleep. There was no doubt he was ex-military too. Marco moved farther back and took a seat on the opposite side from Spook, keeping him with in eyesight. Gage took the seat across the aisle.

It wasn't long before they started moving and were in the air. Henry banked back toward the east. He climbed above the clouds and called back over the speaker about their arrival time and the weather conditions there in the air and on the ground when they landed.

When the intercom clicked off Gage engaged in a conversation with Marco, learning all he could about the men they were going up against in a city that Marco grew up in. Spook only looked over his shoulder once, then reached for a computer and opened it up and began working on info from the Lattimers.

Chapter 19

Despite her efforts to stay awake, JJ fell into a light doze. She eventually woke in the early hours of the morning. The sandwich was still on the nightstand as was the candy bar. She carefully opened the candy, not trusting a sandwich which had sat out all night. The sweetness of the chocolate along with caramel and nuts helped get her going. After several bites and a drink of water, JJ carefully slid off the bed and peered into the other room, the same two men were slouched down in the sofa, sleeping. The television was still on. An empty pizza box and beer cans were all over the coffee table; more cans had toppled over and landed on the floor. She doubted if they would wake feeling all that well.

JJ silently stepped into that room taking in all of the details. As she had expected, it was just a small suite: living area, kitchenette, bathroom and the bedroom she was in. She glanced toward the door, wanting to leave, but not knowing what was on the other side. Better to stay here in one place and let Dennis come to her. Shaking her head, she made her way to the bathroom to freshen up. Going back to the window, she took a better look at her surroundings, trying to figure out exactly where she was.

Nothing looked familiar! She couldn't distinguish any landmarks, so she wasn't at all sure what city she was in. Really looking around, JJ hoped to find something to remember the area by, just in case she was able to get away. She was too high up in the building to be able to read the street signs. Whoever chose this location, knew what they were doing. JJ couldn't even see a sign, like the name of a company, on any of the buildings surrounding this one. Disappointed, she turned away from the window.

JJ went to the chair sitting in the corner of the bedroom. She would sit, quietly and wait until the two men in the other room woke up. She wondered how long it would be before Dennis found her. Clearly, she had been gone more than eighteen hours. It was midmorning yesterday when she was standing outside of her building wondering about her future. She was kicking herself for refusing one of the men to walk her back inside. All she had wanted was a few minutes to come to terms that her life there had come to an end.

But how had they found her? Marco said he was the only one besides her father who knew about her. Evidently, someone had been keeping tabs on Marco while he was keeping tabs on her. Marco claimed he was protecting her, but to have her taken right in front of him would probably send her father over the edge and have Marco in a bad way, perhaps even killed. If her father had other plans for her as Dennis suspected, did this really complicate matters?

Dennis carefully read through the material he had just gotten from the Lattimers. He reread through it, highlighting and taking notes, then read it again. JJ's father was one mean son of a bitch. As they had been told before, he was under suspicion of personally murdering not only JJ's mother, but three other individuals. He was also a key to the disappearance of too many witnesses and jury members. The justice department just couldn't prove any of it. When they had a witness, said witness would mysteriously disappear. How the hell had a man like Giovanni kept alluding law enforcement was beyond Dennis; unless he had them in his pocket. At some point, a man like Giovanni got over confident, thinking he was untouchable. If he knew anything, Dennis figured that the man needed to see the inside of a coffin himself just for the anguish he put JJ through.

Henry came over the intercom telling them they would be landing at a private airstrip in a few minutes, so please prepare themselves. Dennis glanced over at Thumper and Michaella. Sleeping, she was using his shoulder as a pillow and her left arm across his midsection in a hug. Her other hand was clasped with his as he had his head back sleeping and simply enjoying having her there. Never really believing in the soul mate thing until now, looking at his best friend and the woman he was lucky to call his fiancé, Dennis was wondering if perhaps this could be himself soon.

Shaking his head, he thought they would have to find JJ first. He tapped Thumper on the elbow to wake him. Dennis stored the computer in his bag before turning to look back at Gage and Marco. Dennis had blocked out their conversational tones long ago, but knowing Gage, he got as much information as was possible from the man. No doubt he would also have a plan already forming.

A notification on Dennis's phone had him turning back forward. The Lattimers would meet them at the airstrip with transportation for all of them. Dennis was anxious to talk to them and to find JJ.

JJ was startled out of her thoughts by a phone that rang in the other room. On the fourth ring, Woody answered. After listening, he shoved the other man to wake up. JJ watched as both men stood, stretched, and looked back at her. Woody went to the bathroom while the other man kicked a few cans aside to walk to the window. When Woody came out, the other man entered. JJ still hadn't moved, but watched intently. After the other man left the bathroom, they both moved toward her.

"Get up, we're leaving! Don't try anything and we won't have to hurt you!" Woody said with a stern look.

Slowly, JJ got to her feet, watching both men carefully. Taking wary steps, JJ moved toward the two men. Her arm was taken by the one she didn't know the name of, while Woody opened the door and looked both ways down the hall. They ushered her to the elevator, waiting for the doors to open. Entering, Woody punched the button for the lobby. When they walked out of the elevator, they were joined by two more men. JJ's hopes of making a run for it just evaporated. Taking her out the back door, she was escorted toward a waiting black SUV with darkened windows.

Shivering because JJ didn't have a coat on, she realizing the weather had chilled and the nippy conditions reminded her of the date as being mid-November. How had the days gotten away from her?

No name man opened the back door before taking the shot gun seat, the one other went around to the driver's seat. After JJ got in, Woody got in and the last man slid in from the other side, sandwiching her in the back seat.

Watching the scenery go by, JJ was worried as to where they were taking her. Fifteen minutes later, they pulled into another hotel and she was taken to another non-descript suite. This one was bigger with a complete kitchen and what looked like more bedrooms. Off to one side was a table laden with breakfast foods. Taking a few steps in, JJ watched as three of the men went to the table while the fourth stood at the door.

Although she was hungry, JJ moved around toward the bedroom side of the suite, avoiding looking at the men who now seemed to be her new jailors. Strange that they had bound her when she was unconscious, but now let her move around the suite. Woody' warning was supposedly enough to keep her in line. Apparently, these men didn't think women were capable of anything more than cooking and cleaning. She would bide her time and be a good girl.

JJ looked into the first bedroom and dismissed it immediately: no window. The second was the same, but the third had a window and private bath. She had no idea how long she would be here; it didn't really matter, but she would not share a bathroom with these men.

Woody came to the door, "Come and get something to eat!"

It wasn't a request, just an all-out demand. JJ turned to give him a look that told him she wasn't used to be ordered around. He just gave her the same look as before, standing to the side to let her pass by him to the dining area. The other men had evidently had already finished and three of them had left, leaving only Woody to stay with her. She wouldn't question him, just glad that they were alone. She did have to wonder if they were truly alone or if one or more stood guard outside the room.

Taking a plate, JJ helped herself to some eggs, bacon and fruit. There was a carafe of coffee and it did smell wonderful. Pouring a cup, she took it and her plate to the table. Before she could sit down, Woody held her chair for her and handed her silverware. Such manners for a guard. She ate in silence, trying to ignore him while he drank coffee and watched her.

After finishing her meal, she took her dishes to the kitchen, something none of the others had done. Since there was a dishwasher, JJ put her things in it. She turned back to the table laden with uneaten food. Not knowing what else to do, she started to clean up. She knew she was better off keeping busy than thinking about her new situation.

The fruit was easily put back in their containers. She pondered about the eggs and meats left over. The meat could be reheated and eaten. Not sure about the reheating of the eggs, she dumped them in the garbage. She did the same with the toast. There were some hash browns, which she decided to keep. Once the food had been taken care of, JJ turned to clean up the men's dirty dishes only to find them cleared from the table and sitting by the side of the sink. Giving him a quick look of thanks, JJ loaded them into the dishwasher.

"If you would like to shower, there are some clothes over there that should be suitable for you." Woody pointed to bags sitting next to the couch.

JJ hadn't seen them earlier, so was surprised it had been thought of. "Thank you, I think that would be nice." She wasn't sure why she was being so cordial. It wasn't like she was really a guest.

Gathering the bags, she walked to the larger bedroom. Looking back at him, she closed the door and locked it. Dumping the bags, JJ pawed through the items, surprised they were top of the line brands and styles, and all in her size. She took a complete outfit and went into the bathroom; once again locking the door.

Chapter 20

Dennis was up and out of his seat almost before the plane stopped. He had the door open and the steps down, shooting out to the waiting car and the men standing by it. He was deep into a conversation when the others had left the plane. Not wanting to wait any longer, he quickly made the introductions while herding everyone toward the waiting cars.

The Lattimers were friendly enough, but Dennis had other things on his mind. JJ had to be terrified. She had been afraid of her father, but to be taken right away from her own apartment building while they were supposed to be protecting her, had to have her wondering just what kind of security people they were.

Getting into the shotgun seat with Nate, Dennis didn't even look to see the others give him a peculiar shake of their heads. Thumper knew where he was coming from, as did Gage. The other man from the plane got in with Spook along with Gage.

Marco wasn't about to be in the same ride with Dennis, so walked with Michaella and Thumper to the second vehicle with Nick. Knowing they were meeting brothers was one thing, but to be looking at identical twins was unusual to say the least and almost creepy since it was hard to really tell them apart. Marco had never had the pleasure of meeting twins, and to have two of them working in their current capacity was intriguing.

Watching the scenery go by didn't help Dennis in the least. Nate had told him that they had been monitoring the beacon, which had been stationary since getting to New York. It showed that she was in an upscale hotel in a very ritzy part on town. They couldn't determine what floor she was on, yet at this point, hadn't moved out of the building. Nate had given Dennis a computer once in the car, pulling up the same type of program Dennis had on his own computer and phone. They talked only briefly, Dennis only had one thing on his mind: getting JJ out and back with him.

It was the wee hours of the morning when they checked into a hotel across the street from the one where JJ was. They were on the lowest floor possible so they could leave quickly if necessary. The Lattimers had gotten three rooms for them: Thumper and Michaella in one, Gage and Marco in the second one and Dennis and Reed in the third. Dennis took advantage of the shower and started the mini coffee pot after dropping his duffel on the floor.

When he came out, the coffee was ready and Reed was already working on his first cup. Dennis gave him a look which gained him only a big smile. If Reed was anything, it was always positive. He wasn't sure why Gage had called him, but was glad he was there with them. It was comforting having most of their team back together.

Grabbing a cup of coffee, Dennis was checking his phone for JJ's location. She was still in the hotel across the street.

"Spook, get some sleep." Reed said. "I'll take the first watch and wake you if there is a change. Until the Lattimers gather more intel and we have a plan formulated, we can't rush in and get her."

Dennis was reluctant to sleep; there was no telling what was going on in the room where JJ was. He gave a nod and stretched out on a bed. His military training was deeply etched in his soul and he was sleeping within seconds, knowing he would wake immediately if someone said his name.

Barely two hours later Reed said, "Spook, they're moving her."

Dennis was up and on his feet, moving toward the door and down the hall. If he could get a chance to see her and how many people they were dealing with, perhaps they could make their move now. He waited on the street, with Thumper and Gage coming out just as fast as Doc had knocked on their doors.

They waited, watching for them to come out the lobby door. After fifteen minutes, Dennis pulled his phone out and brought up the tracking app.

"Fuck!" He exclaimed while he raced for the truck. "They must have taken her out the back!" he yelled.

The others also sprinted toward the waiting truck. Starting the truck as the last door closed, they tore around the corner. With Thumper in the shotgun seat, he took Spook's phone to direct him. They were several blocks away, but didn't have a problem catching up. After fifteen minutes, the SUV pulled into another hotel. Spook stopped across the street and watched as four men and JJ got out of the SUV and went in the front door.

He watched as JJ tried to look around, but the size of the men surrounding her made that impossible. Dennis sent a mental prayer and thought toward her, hoping she could feel his presence.
She gave one last look in their direction before being whisked into the hotel.

Thumper was already on his own phone, snapping pictures then calling the Lattimers, giving them the new location. Dennis knew Thumper would send the pics to all of them, along with Geek and the Lattimers. Damn! This was just another twist in their attempt to get JJ back. They first would have to figure out who they were dealing with. What angle did these guys have to take Giovanni's daughter?

It was time for Marco to start helping them out and use his knowledge of his boss and this city. It was time for that man and the one who had JJ taken to go down. With Marco's knowledge, the Lattimers intel and their military experience, it was time to knock down this crime group.

JJ unlocked the door and came out of the bedroom to find that she was still alone with Woody. She looked around and gave him a questioning glance. Taking the time to really think things over, she

113

walked to the clean table and sat down. She would give anything for her phone or computer, but knew better than to ask.

"Woody, would it be too much to ask for some books or something for me to read?"

Turning from the TV, he just shrugged and took his phone from his pocket. "What kind of books? Or would magazines do?"

Studying him, she wondered if there were any real brain cells in his head, because most people knew magazines were only advertisements. "Books please. Anything fiction, not Sci-Fi though."

Giving a shake of his head, he sent a text to someone, closed his phone and went back to his TV.

"Well," she stood and moved toward him, "How long will it take? If you plan to keep me here, I have to have something thing to do. If not, I may take to thinking of ways to make your life hell and scheming a way to get out of here."

For several seconds, he watched the TV then looked up at her. She was trying to intimidate him, he thought, interesting.

"They should be here in a few minutes. Don't get your panties in a wad!"

That set her off, "You have no clue about me! Don't try to patronize me!"

While she was at it, she might as well try and get some information about where she was and what she was doing here. Pacing around the room, she started to gather her thoughts.

"Woody, where am I anyway? Who is your boss, is it Giovanni? If it's not, you are in a lot of trouble. I don't think he will take it too well that you have taken me and are holding me against my will."

He didn't even acknowledge that she had said anything. Instead, just continued to be engrossed by what he was watching. Well, if he was going to ignore her, she would take this time to investigate her surroundings.

She stepped back to the kitchen, opening every drawer and cupboard looking for anything she could use as a weapon. They must have thought of that as all she could find were butter knives, spoons, forks and other dull cooking utensils. She speculated they had thought about that and removed all of the sharp kitchen tools. The cupboards had a lot of junk food and the fridge was stocked mostly with beer, sodas and sandwich fixings.

Apparently, she would be here for a while. That was the best conclusion she could come up with. Staying put in one location and not being moved would make it easier for Dennis and Paul to find her and get her out. She hoped that it wouldn't take too long.

Chapter 21

Thumper suggested they go back to their hotel and make some plans. Spook wasn't about to leave again and take the chance the kidnappers move her while they were gone. There was a coffee shop across the street and he was going to camp out there and stay close. Thumper and Gage exchanged looks, nodded and decided they wouldn't be able to talk him out of it. Thumper understood completely since he had gone through something like this only a short time ago. Being helpless while someone you loved was in peril had almost brought him to his knees and he had already accepted the fact that he loved Michaella. Spook cared deeply for JJ, Thumper could see, but did he realize yet that he was in love with her?

Thumper watched as Spook crossed the street, enter the coffee shop and order a large coffee. Taking the cup and grabbing a paper, he moved to a seat by the window and got comfortable. Most would think he was engrossed in an article, but he knew his friend better than anyone else. Spook was the most vigilant person on their team; it was said he knew when an ant moved on the jungle floor and what direction it would be going. Thumper chuckled before turning back to Gage.

"Let's go back to the hotel, get the Lattimers and Geek working on the photos and the SUV and see if we can figure out who we are dealing with." He moved around to the driver's door and took one last look at Spook. They exchanged a look, a nod and a silent agreement. Gage knew not to ask. His men were more brothers than team members. Most people wouldn't understand the bond between his team. Gage got in the shotgun seat and they drove off.

After pacing for twenty minutes, JJ was about to ask again when the door opened and one of the men from earlier brought in a bag and shoved it at her. She quickly looked and saw it was full of new paperback books. As she was about to thank him, he was already closing the door behind him, leaving as fast as he had entered.

JJ took the bag into the room she had chosen and dumped them on the bed. Most were romances, with a few thrillers thrown in. There had to be twenty or more. Shaking her head, she started to organize them, reading the back of each and setting them on the dresser in order she wanted to read them. Taking the first, JJ made her way to the big wing back chair in the corner. She made herself comfortable and turned to the first page.

Several hours later, Woody came and knocked on the door frame. JJ looked up to acknowledge him.

"Dinner is here," he said gruffly. "Come and eat while it's still hot." With that he turned and walked away.

JJ looked for something to mark her spot. She didn't see anything so just dog-eared the page and put the book down on the night stand. Seeing the Chinese cartons sitting on the table, she walked into the kitchen and found a plate and fork. She looked at all of the food and wondered if others were joining them. She hadn't realized she had asked it out loud until Woody said, no.

Making her plate, taking a bottle of water, JJ glanced at Woody sitting on the couch still watching TV. He had several take-out containers on the table in front of him and one in his hand. She shook her head and went to her room, closing the door this time. There was no way she wanted to share meal time with him or anyone else for that matter. She would have liked some light music, but there weren't any electronic devices of any kind in the bedroom. The only TV was in the living area which was strange, she thought.

When the sun was down, she left her bedroom to take her plate back to the kitchen. She wasn't surprised to see that all of the food was still sitting on the table. JJ started to clean up, then stopped, deciding she wasn't a guest or even the hostess. Let someone else do it! She put her plate in the sink, grabbed another water and some cookies she saw in one of the cupboards. Going back to her room, she didn't bother looking at her jailor.

With the door closed and carefully locked, she didn't want to be interrupted as she once again searched the room. JJ checked the chair she had sat in, digging down in between the cushion and arms, even lifting the cushion. Getting down on the floor she ran her hands over the thick carpet, wall to wall, looked under the bed, behind the dresser and night stands. She opened every drawer, feeling every inch and edge. Next was the armoire. She was surprised to actually see the metal hangers in it, along with the iron and an ironing board. Taking one of the hangers, she slid it into her bed, under her pillow.

Now on to the bathroom. She did as she had done in the last hotel: pulled every drawer and searched it completely. JJ was about to give up when she spotted something shiny in the back of the space under the sink. She had to work to get it out and was pleased to find a broken screwdriver. It was only the shaft and flat head portion; it was better than nothing.

Going back to sit on the bed, JJ felt better knowing she had three objects she could possibly use as weapons. A razor blade, hanger and now the screwdriver head. She would do what she could to hide them on her person, well the razor and the screwdriver. There was no way she could hide a hanger.

As she sat on the bed looking at the books, she decided one of them would be the perfect place to hide something. She took the biggest one and decided the binding would be big enough for the screwdriver. Carefully, she pushed it up between the pages and the binding. Once that was done, she laid it by the bed, close within reach. Next, JJ tucked the razor in the book she was reading. She could easily move it from book to book.

There was nothing more she could do now but wait. She settled on the chair with the book she had started earlier and picked up where she had left off. Several hours later, finishing that book, she made herself ready for bed and turned off the light. JJ lay awake quite a while knowing that if Dennis didn't come soon, he may never find her. She even wondered if the trackers still worked, but wouldn't take them off, just to remember him by.

Dennis was accepting his third large cup of coffee and a second sandwich he had ordered when his phone alerted him to a call. After the waitress left, he swiped and answered Thumper's call.

"What have you got?" As a way of greeting, it was rude however as friends and team members, Dennis knew that Thumper didn't expect cordial chatter at the time.

"Marco was able to identify the men from this morning's pictures. They are from a rival of Giovanni and Watters, who was to be given JJ. He said the leader, Caruso, is young and has recently taken over for his ailing father. He wanted to make a name for himself and prove to his father's men he was indeed ready to be the new leader of the family."

Dennis thought this over briefly before speaking, "Does Marco have any idea how this Caruso found out about JJ?"

The moment the question was asked, Spook knew he was on speaker phone. What he heard was muffled only slightly, but he was able to pick up a few voices and knew the Lattimers were also there.

"Marco isn't sure, but said that Watters has a big mouth and probably bragged that he would be getting something very valuable from Giovanni. From there, it undoubtedly spread. There are a lot of people who would like to see Giovanni fall, by whatever means possible." Thumper stopped briefly, listening to someone on the other end. "Spook, has there been any movement there?"

"Not really, one of the goons went to the book store next to the coffee shop and came out with a bag laden with books. He went back to the hotel and came back about ten minutes later. Then about an hour ago, a Chinese delivery came and the man on the street checked the bags and sent the delivery up. Since then nothing."

"Okay, Nick is going to sit on Giovanni's doorstep and Nate will do the same to Watters. Marco and I will go and check out this Caruso and report back to Gage. Since the arrangement to hand JJ over, according to Marco, wasn't supposed to happen for a couple of days yet, we should have plenty of time to get her out. Fortunately, this Caruso has only a few loyal followers; they may be the ones watching JJ. We should be able to take them out easily enough."

Spook thought about this before answering, "If he only has a few men, and it looks like four of them are here, why don't we just slip in and take her out now. With the Lattimers, you, me and Gage it shouldn't be an issue. We could go in and be out before they even knew what hit them."

His comments were met with silence. Spook didn't like it. He was about to end the call when Gage came on the line. "Spook, do you think you can get in the hotel and find out what room she is in?"

"Not a problem!" Spook was ready to do just that when Gage came back.

"Give us thirty minutes to grab something to eat and head over there. The Lattimers will stay on point with Giovanni and Watters."

Spook looked at his watch, "Thirty minutes starting now. If you aren't here by then, I'm going in alone." He ended the call.

Eating his sandwich as quickly as possible, Spook gathered his trash, left a twenty on the table for the waitress and walked out of the coffee shop. It didn't take much to find the men out front. They were sitting in the same SUV, one sleeping and the other reading a newspaper. He pulled a beacon out of his pocket and tapped it to the rear of the rig as he walked by. Then he crossed the street to the hotel. Glancing in one of the windows, he saw a small lobby with a few chairs and the check in counter with only one clerk. Where were the other two; in the room with JJ, or in the hall? He walked to the souvenir shop next to the hotel and looked at a few racks while he waited for the others to arrive.

Spook checked his watch as he saw the others pull up. Thumper, Gage and Reed got out of the car and entered the hotel. He left the store and walked in behind them. Reed went to the desk to distract the desk clerk, Gage sat in a chair while he and Thumper went to the stairwell. Going floor by floor, they finally got the strongest signal on the fourteenth floor. They casually walked down the hall to pin point exactly what room she was in. She was in the middle of the hall, on the opposite side of the building where the two sat in the SUV. There wasn't anyone in the hall, so that meant either both were in the room or one was somewhere else.

Thumper figured maybe out back so he headed back down, taking the elevator this time. He gave a signal to Gage as he exited and went to the back. Reed turned and went to sit with Gage. After several minutes Thumper returned to sit with the other men. He took out his phone, sending a text message to Spook that the fourth man was taking a much-needed nap out back.

"Let's go!" Thumper said.

Gage, Reed and Thumper all walked out the door, got back in their car and drove around to the back to wait for Spook.

Chapter 22

After reading the text from Thumper, Spook slowly made his way toward the room he suspected JJ was in. There hadn't been any activity in the hall, which was in his favor. He checked the time and hoped the later hour would make the man on the other side of the door careless. Knocking quickly, he stepped aside so that he wouldn't be seen through the peep hole. No one answered so he knocked lightly again. It took several minutes before the door opened. Once it did, Spook stepped around and caught the man by surprise with a quick upper cut to the jaw. Stumbling backward, Spook followed him in and quickly hitting him again before closing the door.

The man wasn't about to go down with two hard hits to the face. Regaining his balance, he took a step forward to take the offensive against his attacker. Woody looked at the man who had hit him twice and figured he had it made as he had at least twenty pounds on the man and several inches.

That was Woody's first mistake! Spook smiled, prodding the brute on. Second mistake made; Woody took the bait. He stepped forward both fists raised and ready to start throwing punches. Spook side stepped with the first swing and caught the man in the kidneys with a fast punch before catching him around the neck in a sleeper hold to immobilize, not kill him.

Although he was at a height and weight disadvantage, Spook held on for all he was worth. He needed this guy to go down, and go down fast without making too much noise. The less noise, the less likely they would be interrupted by hotel security or the police. It took longer than expected, but he finely felt the guy collapse. Laying him out on the floor, he wondered if he should tie the goon up, but didn't want to take the time.

Assessing the suite, he noticed that only one door was closed. Quietly, he stepped to the door. He tried the door and found it locked. Removing a small kit from his back pocket, he quickly worked the lock, popping it and put his kit back. He opened the door slowly and as quietly as possible. Spook was relieved to see JJ laying on the bed, sound asleep. Carefully, he sat on the bed next to her and spoke her name. He didn't want to startle her by shaking her awake, but they had to get moving. Again, he said her name and this time she opened her eyes and looked at him.

JJ couldn't believe what she was seeing! Dennis was there sitting on the bed. She blinked a few times just to make sure it wasn't a dream. When she was sure, JJ threw herself into his arms.

"You came! I wasn't so sure you would be able to find me!" She kept her voice low, not wanting Woody to hear her.

Dennis rubbed her back to offer her and himself comfort that she was okay. "Of course, I came. Are you alright? They didn't hurt you, did they?"

He held her back now to get a better look at her.

"No, they had tied me up. When I woke up and asked to use the bathroom, they cut the bonds and told me to be good or they would go back on." She paused and looked into his serious yet strikingly grey eyes. "Dennis, where are we?"

Smiling, he said, "Get dressed, and I will tell you everything once we are out of here."

He stood, holding a hand out to help her up. When she was standing, he took the opportunity to really look into those eyes. Brushing her hair back with both hands, he took her face gently and kissed her. She responded with the passion he already knew was there. He broke the embrace, holding her at arm's length.

JJ smiled before turning and grabbing some of the new clothes still on a chair. She didn't even hesitate to be shy about changing in front of him. Off went the pajamas and on went jeans and a top. She grabbed her shoes and sat down to quickly pull them on. JJ looked around the room and wondered if she was forgetting anything. Glancing at the books, she dismissed them and went to Dennis.

Wrapping her arms around him, she said, "Thank you for coming for me! Now, let's get out of here."

Dennis felt the shiver run through her and hugged her tighter. She felt so good in his arms. He released one arm, tipping her chin up with that hand and kissed her. Stunned, it took her a second to return it with all of the affection and relief she felt toward him.

"Let's go, Thumper is waiting out back for us!" Not wanting to let go of her, he turned her toward the door where her guard lay on the floor, still out cold.

JJ looked down at Woody, "He isn't . . ." She had a hard time getting the word out. "Dead?"

"No, just unconscious." Dennis said as he opened the door, made a quick look both ways down the hall and ushered her out the door.

They never looked back as they headed down the hall to the stairwell. Just as he said, there were men waiting for them in a SUV. Paul got out and opened the door for her with a huge smile. She knew Paul so smiled back at him. Extending his hand to her, he helped her up into the big rig, got in and closed the door while Spook went around to the other side effectively sandwiching her in between the two men. Once they were all in the car, the driver took off knowing exactly where he was going.

JJ relaxed against Dennis, wrapping her hand around his arm. He flexed the muscles she held and turned to smile at her. He, himself, could now relax since they had found her, she was safe and unharmed. Dennis was torn between putting her on the jet and getting her out of the city or locking them in a room and making love to her for several days. For sure, as much as he wanted, he couldn't do the latter.

Gage turned from the shotgun seat, holding out his hand to

introduce himself. "Hello, JJ! I'm Gage and the driver is Reed. We are pleased to meet you, finally."

JJ reached over and shook his hand with a smile. "Gage, thank you for your help getting me out of there."

Gage chuckled and winked at her before nodding to Spook. "Dear, I was just here for the ride. Spook and Thumper did most of the work in finding you."

They pulled into an underground parking ramp. JJ looked around and was a little surprised at where they were. She was sure that she was safe, knowing Dennis wouldn't risk taking her anywhere where there might be a problem.

Reed pulled into a spot near the door and the men got out of the vehicle. Dennis waited for her to come out on his side, pulling her protectively next to him. They all walked toward the door. Reed opened it and they took the few steps up to the lobby floor. Moving toward the elevator, Gage punched the up button and the doors opened for them.

They rode up in complete silence. When the doors opened, Gage, Reed and Thumper went to the left while Dennis steered her to the right, down several doors before he drew her into a room. As soon as the door was closed, and locked with the dead bolt, JJ was pulled into strong arms and backed up against the secured door.

Dennis couldn't wait a second longer to kiss her and she answered in kind. The bruising kiss took all control away from Dennis, much to his own surprise. His hands went from her face, down her neck to her shoulders. He couldn't stop there!

Having to feel her, his hand went to the hem of her shirt she had pulled on in front of him only minutes ago. Tugging it up and over her head, he tossed it aside and just looked at her. She was perfection! Moving his eyes back to hers, Dennis saw the same raw need her eyes which he felt. Not needing anything more than that, he picked her up and carried her to the bed.

Before they had gotten there, JJ was tugging at the back of Dennis's shirt, trying to get it untucked from his jeans. When the tails were free, she ran her hands up and down his back feeling the skin and muscles twitch under them. But she wanted more! Reaching around, she tugged hard enough at the front of the shirt that the snaps popped open revealing his sculptured chest. Pushing the shirt from his shoulders, she leaned forward to smell then kiss the middle of it.

Dennis moved forward enough to ease them both down onto the bed. Once there, he proceeded to kiss every inch of her, removing clothing as he went. His desperate greed for her took control away from him and gave it to her. The taste of her sparked a fire in him, driving him on. There was nothing he wanted more than to make her his, and he knew she wanted the same. His hands plundered and his mouth conquered until they were both in need of that final connection.

He broke off the kisses and touches only long enough to see if she was truly with him. The need and longing in her eyes told him all he needed to know. Carefully, as gently as he was able to considering his own need, he positioned himself at her entrance. While watching her eyes, he pushed slowly into her, encountering her maidenhead. Dennis had never been with a virgin before, but knew that there would be some pain to her.

JJ took a deep breath as she felt Dennis enter her. She knew he was being careful with her virginity, so to reassure him, she adjusted her pelvis and he slid deeper into her, breaking through at last. He stopped to give her more time to become accustom to his intrusion. Bending down he started to kiss her again.

When he felt her arching up toward him, he began moving again. Dennis wanted to make sure that her first time was the most pleasurable, so he would work hard to make sure she came at least once before he took his own pleasure. As he felt her contract, grip him tightly and waited for her to come down before taking her back up. After her third climb and tumble, he took his own pleasure and came with her.

He collapsed on her, trying to bring his breathing back to normal. Knowing he was heavy was one thing, doing anything about it was another. When he could, Dennis rolled over and brought her next to him, wrapping his arms around her.

JJ sighed. She had no other way to express herself any further than that. Dennis reached down and pulled covers over them. As he stroked her back, she dropped into sleep, with him following shortly afterward.

Early the next morning, Dennis was coming out of the bathroom ready for the day, when there was a light rap on the door. He first looked toward the bed where JJ still lay sleeping. Then looking out the peep hole and seeing Thumper and Michaella, he stepped out into the hall. He didn't want to disturb his sleeping beauty; she needed the sleep.

"Morning!" he said as he eyed his friends.

Michaella held a small bag, "I figured JJ could use some new clothes and toiletries."

Dennis took the bag and almost made it back into the room before Thumper stopped him.

"Gage has a room for all of us to have breakfast and go over what we should do now."

Judging by the tone of his voice, they would need to be there. So, Dennis asked, "What time?"

Thumper smiled, "Just to give JJ a little time, he thought nine would be good. You in?"

"We'll be there. She's still sleeping. I'll get her up in a little bit. Thanks for the clothes, she will appreciate it a lot."

With that, he turned and went back into their room. A quick glance told him, JJ was still sleeping, so he went to the table and sat down and brought up his computer. Swiftly, Dennis browsed through his email finding a message from the Lattimers he opened and read all of the update info they had. They had made sure the men who took JJ were taken into custody by the local cops. He was sure they would go over this at the meeting. After reading more email, he checked the time and found he had lost track of time.

Carefully, Dennis went to the bed, sitting down next to JJ. She never looked more beautiful to him, peaceful in sleep. He hated to wake her, however, knew she would want to shower before they left the room. Very tenderly, he placed his hand on her shoulder and before he could shake her, she opened her eyes.

JJ smiled at him, nearly causing him to lose himself in her once more. There would be time for that later, after she was completely safe from her father.

"Good morning, beautiful!" he said before he leaned over and gave her a light morning kiss.

"Good morning back! How long have you been up?" JJ asked as she stretched to relieve the sleeping kinks. The sheet fell away from her naked body and Dennis knew he better move before he couldn't.

"A little while. Mic brought some new clothes over and Gage has a breakfast in a private room planned."

Tossing the sheet and blanket off, JJ swung her feet around and dropped them to the floor, standing in a graceful move. Once again, she stretched. Dennis groaned as he watched her move her body, one very fine and naked body, before him. After their lovemaking, all of her shyness toward him was gone. Of that he was glad, they connected on every level before last night and now they were connected physically too.

"You better go shower, or I may drag you back to bed." He said it with a sexy grin meaning every word of it.

Taking him at his word, she moved toward him, brushed her lips across his then headed to the bathroom. Snagging the bag from the bed, JJ took them to the bathroom with her. Michaella knew her size and style, she smiled as she removed clean under garments, new jeans and a lovely, soft sweater. She turned on the water in the shower, relieved herself then stepped into the tub and almost purred as the hot water hit her. They had made love several times during the night; she was slightly sore, in a good way. She almost smirked knowing that her father had kept boys and men away from her so she would retain her virginity. Now it didn't matter!

After washing and conditioning her hair, she lathered her body and rinsed. Toweling off, JJ wondered what the meeting would be about. Now that she was safe, she just wanted out of this city and away from her father, never to be seen by him ever again. She found a brush and other womanly essentials in the bag so took full advantage of them.

When JJ came out of the bathroom, wearing new clothes and feeling like a new woman, she stopped to get Dennis's approval. Coming around the corner, she looked toward the table where he was putting his computer and other items in a satchel. Dennis looked up and was stunned! He set his bag down and came toward her with the grace and silence of a panther seeking its prey.

Dennis stepped to her, their toes almost touching. He looked down at her and knew there wasn't another woman for him. He had found her, finally. Cupping her face with both hands his claimed her mouth.

"You look gorgeous!" Resting his forehead on hers, he sighed. "We better go before I lose my control and take you back to bed."

Smiling at her, he released her face, but kept one hand in his while the other snatched up his bag. They headed out the door and down the hall to the elevator.

Chapter 23

As they entered the meeting room, JJ was hit with the aroma of fresh coffee. Releasing a small whimper, she headed toward the tall server with cups all around it. She made herself a cup and took that first drink. She hadn't realized everyone was watching until she was nearly finished with her first cup. She looked up and smiled at everyone with a 'what' look, before making a second cup.

Taking her cup, JJ went to where Michaella was sitting. As she approached, her best friend got up and took her in a hug which almost took her breath away.

"I was so worried about you," Michaella said. "You scared me half to death. I'm glad you are safe and unharmed." Michaella released her and stepped back to really look at JJ.

JJ was stunned, "Thank you for being here and thanks for the clothes!" Her shyness came out now.

Dennis came over, followed by two very handsome and identical looking men. Stopping next to her, he introduced them.

"JJ, I would like you to meet Nick and Nate Lattimer. They work for the . . ." he stopped not exactly what agency they worked for. "They work for the government. They were instrumental in aiding us to find you."

JJ looked at each one several times with confusion on her face. Which was which?

"I'm Nate," the first said, smiled and looked at his brother. "I'm the handsome one. This is my brother Nick."

Nick elbowed his brother with a smile on his face, "Pleased to meet you. We're glad that you are okay and didn't get hurt."

JJ extended her hand to greet each man, still stunned by their good looks. "Thank you for helping Dennis find me. I don't know how to repay you for that."

Sensing her embarrassment, Dennis pulled out a chair for her to sit down. Within minutes the table was filled and food was brought out. The conversation during breakfast was light, easy and full of laughter and jokes. When the plates had been cleared and the waitstaff gone, the conversations turned more serious.

JJ listened, taking in all of the information the Lattimers shared. Looking around the table and the others in the room, she spotted Marco sitting with the other two men she had met last night. She hadn't realized that he was here and wondered about it. Apparently, he had information which was helpful and could be used to take her father down.

The government had a lot of info, but nothing solid enough to convict him. She tried to concentrate on the flow of exchanges between everyone but couldn't. JJ kept thinking about the letter her mother had written to her. It had been so long since she had looked at it, that she couldn't remember exactly what was in it.

Getting Dennis's attention by gripping his arm, she said, "Dennis I need to get to some of my things."

"Later," was all he said.

"Dennis, I think I might have something to help put my father away." JJ said it loud enough that all conversation in the room stopped and everyone looked at her.

"Are you sure?" Nick asked.

"When I was sixteen, I needed my birth certificate to get my driver's license. My parents kept ignoring my request for it, so one night when they were out, I went looking for it. I found it along with the adoption papers, a letter to the adoptive parents and one written to me. Mine was in a sealed envelope. I still have all of that paperwork, back with my things." She stopped and looked at Dennis. "I don't remember exactly what was in that envelope, but my mother was afraid, for me and for herself."

Dennis turned completely in his seat now and took both of her hands. "JJ, are you sure?"

Nodding her head yes, she added, "I was so shocked that I had been adopted, that I just scanned over the letters then tucked them away." JJ looked at the others at the table, saw that Marco had stood up to look at her. "We have to go back and get them!"

Looking over at Gage, Dennis wasn't about to let her go anywhere and Gage must have picked up on that.

Gage came over and helped JJ out of her chair. "JJ, if you know where the letters are, I will send someone for them."

Reed was already walking toward her too. She looked at both men, then to Paul and Michaella. Dennis stood and pulled her back to him enclosing her in his arms.

"Tell us where they are; Reed will take the jet back and get them, and come back here with them." Gage said.

Taking relief in Dennis's support, JJ answered as clearly as possible. "They're in the guitar case. I opened the lining under the neck and folded them carefully so no one would notice. Then I glued the lining back down."

JJ had barely finished speaking when Paul tossed keys to Reed and he was out the door with his phone to his ear. She was amazed at men she hardly knew were willing to help her, no questions asked. These new friends were her blessing. She had no idea people would help her other than Michaella.

"Wait, can you bring some of my clothes too?" JJ said loudly and everyone laughed, but Reed was already out the door.

Turning to Dennis, JJ hugged him tight, relief coursing through her. When she looked up at him, she saw something in his eyes she couldn't define. He smiled and she felt the fear fall away. She glanced around the room and noticed how Marco was watching her with Dennis.

Pulling away from him, she walked toward Marco. He seemed uncomfortable all of a sudden, looking down at his own feet.

"Marco," JJ started. She wasn't sure what she wanted to say to him, rage came first. "I'm not sure why you are here, I really don't care. But if you would have been honest and straight with me weeks ago, we wouldn't be here! I wouldn't have been kidnapped and brought to New York, drugged and bound. I would have been able to get away from his reach a lot sooner; he wouldn't have been able to find me."

Dennis had moved to her, putting his hands on her shoulders as support. It was clear that she didn't need anything further from him; Marco was clearly ashamed of himself.

"JJ, I am sorry." Marco searched for the correct words. "I didn't want you hurt, but I didn't know what else to do. I didn't know you were planning on getting away and hiding from your father. I would have done anything to see that you wouldn't be hurt. I didn't know how."

She could see the pain in his features. She also knew he meant every word; she could forgive him because of it.

"Marco was able to help, JJ." Dennis started. "He was able to identify the men who had taken you. Apparently, your father wasn't the only one willing to use you to gain advantage in this city. It was a completely different family behind the kidnapping."

Looking for confirmation, JJ scanned the faces of the other men in the room and saw several nodding their heads. Taking it as a fact, she knew then that she wanted out of this city.

Taking Marco's hand, she quietly said, "Thank you Marco for helping. I will forgive you, if you promise to get away from my father, from this life. Go somewhere and start over. You deserve to have a life where there isn't deceit and betrayal all around you." She smiled at him, which he returned with a nod.

"Thanks JJ! Gage and the Lattimers have assured me that by helping them, I will be able to be put into the witness protection program and given a fresh start." He sheepishly looked at the twins.

JJ wasn't sure what kind of help he was giving them, but truly hoped Marco could live someplace where he wouldn't have to deal with men like her father again.

Gage decided that nothing more could be done until Reed returned, so effectively dismissed everyone to get some rest. Paul and Michaella were going to head to the shops within the hotel and asked JJ if she wanted or needed anything. JJ wished she would have thought more about her own suitcases and which ones she wanted before Reed left, but other than that, just a nap. Gage pulled out his phone and called Reed, adding to the items to be brought back after getting a brief description on JJ's bags and also Michaella's. They all moved to the door.

After following the Lattimers and Marco out, JJ got that feeling once again. She stiffened and stopped just outside the door. She skimmed the hallway in all directions. Dennis came to an instant alert status when he felt her stop.

"Code blue!" he voiced while looking at Thumper and Gage. Both men moved in front of the women, almost pushing them back in the room.

All of a sudden, two men dressed in dark suits came around the corner. The guns in their hands were all that was needed to put everyone in a heightened state of alertness. Michaella and JJ were pushed to the floor with Paul and Dennis covering them, using their own bodies as protection for the women. Nick and Nate had dropped to their knees.

As the Lattimers drew their weapons, two shots were fired in Marco's direction. The first hit him in the left shoulder and the second in his mid-stomach. Marco went down fast. Before the two in the dark suits could fire again, Nick and Nate, with a quick aim, each fired. They hit their targets, directly dead center in the forehead.

Nick and Nate were already policing the area, pushing the gunman's weapons toward the wall out of the way, keeping employees and guests at bay while Paul called *911*. Dennis was pushing Michaella and JJ back into the meeting room, effectively keeping them out of sight. He went in with them, closing the door; to keep them safe and away from curious eyes was essential. Nate took his phone out and was also making a call to his office to get more back up down to the hotel.

Gage started moving toward Marco, crawling across the floor. He pulled his own jacket off to push into the wounds, trying to stop the blood. As soon as Paul was off the phone, he too moved toward Marco. Gage was doing what he could to keep Marco alive, but he was losing too much blood.

Marco was trying to speak, "They were from Giovanni." He was trying to turn his head toward the door where JJ was. "You have to get her out of here. If he found me, he must know she too is in the city."

"Take it easy, you need to stop talking. An ambulance will be here soon." Gage said.

Marco grabbed his arm, looking directly into Gage's face, "Get her out of here, and not just out of the city! You need to get her as far away as possible. Don't let that animal get to her." His breathing was becoming too labored to keep talking. On a final breath, he said, "Please!"

Thumper looked at Gage, then moved toward the meeting room door. With a signal to Spook, he slipped into the room.

"We have to get the women out of here." He spoke quietly. "Marco said the shooters were Giovanni's."

"Fuck!" was all Spook had time to say as they all moved toward the kitchen entrance. Without more back up, they had no chance to leave the building, so they would go back up to one of the rooms until the Lattimers cleared the scene and they could formulate a better plan to get JJ out of the hotel. Once they were in the hall leading to the kitchens, they found the service elevator. Taking it up to the next floor, the men carefully checked the main hotel hall before allowing the women out of the elevator. There were several guests in the hall, but didn't seem to pose a problem. Walking past them, they entered the main stairwell and went up to their floor.

Chapter 24

Once they were in Paul and Michaella's room, the men looked at each other and went to Paul's duffle and pulled out handguns for each of them. Paul wasn't sure why he had packed them, but was more than glad he had. After they had checked the weapons and ammo, they holstered them, securing them on their belts.

JJ and Michaella watched the actions of the men and knew beyond a doubt that it was more than routine for them. JJ couldn't help the feeling of dread that had just came down on them. Marco had been shot protecting her; which meant her father must know they were in the city. She started to shake, and it had nothing to do with her being cold. Collapsing on the bed, JJ sat with her head down. Now what, she thought.

Dennis came over and sat down next to JJ and wrapped her up in a blanket, then his arms. He could feel the tremors wracking her body. He knew from experience some was adrenaline, however, most of it was just plain fear. JJ wasn't used to encountering gun fights, so he knew she was scared. Seeing Marco shot after she had spoken to him, getting his apology couldn't help either. He hoped that Marco would live, although another part of him knew by the looks of the wounds it was not probable.

After fifteen minutes, there was a light, quick knock on the door. Paul went over and looked out the peep hole. Seeing Gage, he quickly opened the door and stepped aside. Gage surveyed the room; Dennis with JJ on the bed and Michaella occupying a chair by the window. He would have preferred to have this conversation with just the men, which would be better on the women. He also knew that the ladies, especially JJ, were in danger here and they needed to hear what he had to say.

"I called Reed and told him to hold at the airport until I called him back." Gage said as he walked over to squat in front of JJ. "Marco didn't make it." He said quietly as he took one of her hands. "His last thoughts were for your safety though, JJ. He told me to protect you, get you out of the city. If your father found out Marco was here, he also knows you are too."

Looking at her, Gage assessed whether she was comprehending his words. JJ gave him a brief, almost undetected nod.

Gage continued, clearly in charge and commander mode. "As I said, I called Reed and he is waiting at the small airstrip where the jet we came in on is waiting. I think we need to get you ladies out of here as soon as possible. We will wait until the Lattimers come up and the scene downstairs is clear. We need back up and a safe way out of the hotel, Giovanni will be watching it for sure now."

A lot of scenarios were going through Dennis's head, trying to formulate a way to get out of here undetected. His thoughts were too jumbled with his feeling for the woman they were trying to protect. He needed to take a walk and check out the building.

Before standing up Dennis said, "Let me take a walk, scope the building, its entrances and the street. There might be a way to leave, but I have to know the terrain first."

Paul and Gage knew of Spook's abilities and no one could get in and out of a situation better than Spook. They each nodded in agreement. Gage stood and stepped back. Dennis gave JJ a squeeze, a swift kiss and got up from the bed.

"Give me about thirty minutes, forty-five tops." He checked his phone, drew on his jacket off a chair and slipped out the door.

JJ watched as Paul went to the door and locked it before going over to Michaella. Without Dennis next to her, she felt really alone. She then tried to process the fact that Marco had died and at her father's hand. He may not have actually pulled the trigger, but his own men were behind the recent attack. She had to get her mind off of that gory detail. She dropped the blanket and stood.

"Gage, Marco had identified the men who had me. How did he do that?"

Gage pulled a chair out and moved it toward the bed and motioned for her to sit. Once she had, he too sat down. "We had gotten pictures when they moved you from the first hotel to the second. We didn't want to charge in to get you at that point since we didn't really know how many men there were, whether they were armed or not. Dennis sent the pictures to the Lattimers, and they showed them to Marco."

Thinking this over, JJ asked, "So, just who were those men, the ones that had me?"

He could see the intelligence in the woman sitting on the bed, actually had admiration for her and courage from what he knew of her. He also knew he couldn't pull any punches; she needed to know, as much as she could, about her own situation.

"A family by the name of Caruso was responsible. The father is ill and the son took over, and to get loyalty and recognition, he thought to take what was promised to Watters. How he had found out about the deal your father made with Watters? Marco said Watters has a big mouth and likes to brag. That got you caught in the middle of a deadly triangle of mob families. All of them wanting to gain more power. Believe me, Jennifer Jean, we will do everything to make sure you are safe. Just like Michaella, you're family now."

With that they both looked toward Michaella and Paul, standing by the window, in each other's arms, looking out. JJ nodded and was more than thankful that Gage gave her the truth.

They all turned toward the door at the short quick coded knock. Gage got up to let Dennis back in. Right on his heels were the Lattimers. It seemed that fate was with them. Dennis smiled as he came toward JJ, retaking the seat he had before he left.

The Lattimers had no new information, the hallway had been

closed off, bodies removed and the hotel staff on alert. Nick had said that there would be four more agents coming in for protection detail. It may not be until later this evening though. Dennis decided to put in his thoughts about moving the women out of the building but wanted to wait until they had more men available.

"I think we could get the ladies out by the service entrance. There are several men watching the front and rear entrances and only one at the delivery door. We will have to devise some kind of disguise or some way to conceal them. Maybe a large moving carton or catering cart. But let's wait until it gets a little later in the day, when the men relax a little and we have more back up."

The room got extremely quiet, so quiet JJ stood and paced the available space thinking. Everyone watched her, but Dennis was the only one who knew she was really thinking, sorting the whole situation in her mind. When she stopped and turned back toward him, he knew he wasn't going to like what came out of her mouth.

"Getting me out of here won't bring my father to justice, will it?" JJ said frankly.

It was Nate who answered her, "No, it won't. Unless your letters have actual proof in them."

"Do you think he knew that I had been taken and who had done it?" she asked.

"We don't know JJ." Nate said. "Possibly? Probably!"

"Any idea how he found out Marco was here?"

Both Lattimers shook their heads, not having an idea how Marco had been found.

She continued, "So, if there were three specific groups in this, why not still pit them against each other?" Looking around to gain Gage's attention, JJ went on. "If the Carusos did this to gain leverage, perhaps we could use that to our favor. I don't want to see any one hurt, but maybe we could get my father and the other group to come out to trade for me, so to speak."

Dennis shot to his feet, "Hell no! We are not using you as bait!" He stalked over to her, making her back up, bumping the wall.

Putting her hand lightly over his heart, she said, "That is not exactly what I meant." She gave him a sincere look, pleading with him to let her finish. "I want out of this as much as you want me out."

"Gage, didn't you say that the young Caruso was looking for loyalty from his own men?"

Realizing where this might be going, he said, "Yes. Go on."

Turning now to the Lattimers, "Have you any reason to believe that maybe they aren't really into the crime world?"

Nick and Nate looked at her and each other then smiled, knowing exactly where her thoughts were going.

"We have reason to believe that with the son taking over, he wanted more and was willing to get in bed with the big, bad boys to expand their business. At this point, we have no evidence they have been into anything illegal." Nick said stepping toward JJ. "You have something on your mind, don't you?"

JJ swallowed, or tried to. Walking to the fridge she took a bottle of water, opened it and took a long drink. Revolving back to the room, she worked through what she wanted to say.

"The men holding me didn't seem like bad men. Woody did what he could to make me comfortable. He could have kept my hands bound, but he didn't. He made sure I had food and a private bathroom and when I asked for something to read, he got it for me. When we got to the second hotel, there was a completely separate room for me with new clothes too. Woody didn't seem like someone that would have intentionally hurt me. I can't say the same for my father. And it doesn't seem like this Watters is a kind man either."

Nick got her attention by touching her arm lightly, "I think I get what you're getting at. Let Nate and I do some digging on the Caruso's son. May I suggest that you get some rest. You look a little tired." He smiled down at her then moved with his brother to the door.

Chapter 25

Dennis waited until he was sure the Lattimers were gone and not likely to return within the next few minutes. Then he walked over to where JJ was standing, taking her hand in his. Her hand was cold and she was looking tired, but he had other plans.

"Gage, Reed is waiting at the air strip and I think that we should get the women out now, not to wait for the Lattimers and their extra men." He got a quick agreeing look from Thumper. "Like JJ pointed out, we don't know how Giovanni found out how Marco was here. As far as I know, the only time I saw him use his phone was after JJ said she wasn't flying here with him. He made a short call and I am betting after she was grabbed, he hadn't had time or privacy to make another. My thoughts are either Giovanni has someone inside the hotel or somewhere in the government. I don't want to wait until the Lattimers get more help here. I think we should move the ladies out right now."

Gage stood, walked to the window. He was sure Spook was right, and the safety of the women was vital first of all and would take a lot of worry out of two of his men.

"I think you're right." Gage agreed. "I'll walk down to the kitchen and see if I can get what we need. You get ready up here, clear out your rooms."

With that Gage turned and left. Thumper started to pack up their items around the room as Dennis tugged JJ toward the door and down the hall. In their room, they grabbed all of their stuff and shoved it into his duffle bag. Dennis policed the room, making sure that nothing whatsoever was left but typical hotel furnishings. When he was sure the room was clear, he took his phone and sent a message to

Gage and Thumper. A quick response came back to meet them back down at the same room they had breakfast in.

As soon as they entered the dining room, Gage appeared with two caterer's jackets which he handed to Paul and Dennis. They slipped them on as the women followed quietly behind him toward the kitchen. Dennis and Paul brought up the rear, watching to make sure they weren't noticed. At the kitchen door, Gage laid out the quick plan giving them the name of the head caterer and where and when the meeting was to be catered.

Gage walked over to a bunch of enclosed carts, motioning to the two open ones. They were big enough for JJ to be comfortable in but would be a squeeze for Michaella. It was a good thing they wouldn't be in them very long. The caterer would pull out of the hotel's lot, head east for six blocks before pulling over to let the four of them out, where they would hail a cab then proceed to the air strip where Reed was waiting for them.

Staying back at the hotel, Gage would wait for the Lattimers to come back and then let them know what had happened, that they didn't feel comfortable waiting for Giovanni or Watters to find out that JJ was there, and there might be a mole or two near enough to bring the heat of another gun fight to them.

Taking a few minutes to say good-byes, Gage first took Michaella in a fatherly hug. He kissed her cheek and then turned to JJ, who had watched the exchange with curiosity. She was surprised when he did the same to her. She was almost embarrassed by the show of affection toward her, since she had only met the man last night. On the other hand, it felt wonderful to have trust in someone when she had gone without for so long.

In her ear he said, "Be safe and don't worry. We won't let anything happen to one of our own."

With that he stepped back and the women stepped into their own little tuna can, along with the men's duffle bags. Dennis and Paul gave their women a quick kiss then pulled down the rolling door before wheeling the carts out to the waiting caterer truck. Dennis went to the front of the truck as Paul got in the back. Gage closed the cargo door, giving it several swift raps that they were good to go. He watched as the truck pulled away from the building and out onto the bustling New York street. When they were out of sight, he made his way back through the hotel and up to the room he had occupied the last few nights to wait for the Lattimers to return.

Several minutes later, JJ felt the truck take a turn then slowed as Paul opened the cart door and she was able to get out of the cramped space. She saw that he had removed the caterer's jacket and was sliding the connecting door open between the cab and cargo space. Dennis squeezed through the small opening, removed the white jacket as soon as the cab door was closed. They still had a few blocks to go before getting out on the street, but it appeared like they had gotten out unnoticed, since Dennis had been watching in his side mirror.

As planned, the truck pulled over and Paul raised the cargo door and making a quick assessment, climbed down from the bed. Dennis then jumped down and looked around. He held his hands out for Michaella and JJ to join them on the street. Then the men grabbed their bags, Paul closed the door and Dennis waved to the driver to continue on. The van pulled away from the curb and Paul whistled for a cab. A yellow minivan pulled up to them and they quickly got in and the cabbie was given the address of the air strip, they were headed out of the downtown area and toward the waiting jet.

Keeping the conversation away from what they were doing and where they were going, Paul would spout something outlandish about the scenery they were driving by or some other factoid about the city. JJ couldn't help but smile and laugh at the knowledge coming from the big and normally quiet man beside Michaella.

Dennis paid the driver, giving him a large tip to forget he had picked them up then sent him on his way. Once they had been dropped off by the terminal where the jet waited for them, Reed came out of the building with the pilot right on his heels. JJ could tell before any words were spoken that the pilot was angry about something.

"What in the hell is going on?"

Dennis spoke to the upset pilot, "We'll talk in the air. How soon can we get wheels up?"

JJ overheard Reed say to Paul, "I can't leave you two alone for five minutes and you're getting into trouble."

Paul just chuckled, and helped Michaella up into the sleek looking jet. He turned and held a hand to JJ, to do the same for her. Once she was in, he looked toward the other men and followed after her. Reed went in next, then Dennis, trailed by the pilot.

JJ took a gasping look around the cabin of the private jet. She was amazed they were actually going to be flying out of New York in this kind of style. Michaella and Paul took two seats next to each other smiling and laughing at something. So JJ took a seat on the other side of the plane but a row behind the couple. Dennis came and sat next to her as she was buckling her seat belt. Reed went to the cockpit with the pilot after the door was closed. Within minutes they were taxiing down the runway and soon were in the air.

Dennis popped open the compartment above his head, grabbed a small pillow and airline sized blanket, handing them to her so he could close the cubby. Covering her with the blanket and slipping the pillow behind her head, he took her hand and closed his own eyes.

JJ rested her head back against the headrest and closed her eyes. She was weary but knew she wouldn't sleep. Marco was dead because of her; well because of her father. If he had just been honest with her it wouldn't have come to this. As a tear trickled down her cheek, Dennis slipped his hand under the blanket and unfastened her seatbelt and pulled her into his lap and let her cry. When the tears ended, he carefully wiped them away and just held her.

He didn't like seeing her hurting; not that he could have really prevented what had happened to Marco. They would see that her father paid for it. Taking a look over at Thumper and Michaella, he saw that they had dozed off too. This might be the best time to talk about what came next.

Carefully, he tipped JJ's face up to look directly into her lovely eyes. "Don't blame yourself for Marco. He made his choice and so did your father. This is on them, not you. Okay?"

She nodded to let him know she'd heard him.

"When we get to Chicago, we will go to the truck and retrieve some of your things. Thumper and I will take the letters back to Gage. You and Michaella will head to her place; where you will be safe. We had a lot of security measures installed when her ex came after her. You will be safe there! The house isn't in Michaella's name and so it can't be linked to you either. Okay?"

Again, all she could do was nod. There was too much which had happened the last few days for her to comprehend anymore, so she laid her head on his shoulder to rest. It hadn't seemed like a long time before he was trying to wake her. When her eyes came open and she knew where she was, he set her back in her seat and tossed the blanket and pillow in the seat next to him.

Minutes later, they were on the ground and walking toward the big SUV that was parked near the building. Reed headed for the driver's door since he had the keys. Thumper gave him the stink eye, Reed just laughed and climbed behind the wheel. The women had the rear doors opened for them then Dennis and Paul jostled for the front seat. JJ and Michaella laughed, Thumper won. Dennis gave him a finger then climbed in beside JJ, taking her hand.

Thumper gave directions to Reed, and little did JJ know but they had the truck moved away from the building. It was in the warehouse next to the decoy truck. Opening the back, Thumper grabbed JJ by the waist and lifted her into the back. When her feet hit the floor, she turned and beamed a thanks to him before moving through her things looking for the one that had her warmer coat in.

The men moved the boxes meant to go with JJ into the pickup bed and JJ sat down with the guitar case. Taking the instrument out, she was about to set it aside when Michaella took it from her. Smiling at her, JJ searched for the seam she had glued so many years ago. She was about to give up, when Dennis produced a pocket knife and handed it to her. With the knife tip, she was able to lift the cloth enough to get the papers and envelope out. With them free she put the guitar back and handed it to Paul to put in the truck.

The papers were thicker than she remembered and as she held the envelope, there was something else in it. JJ opened it and found a small key and a business card with a bank name and address on it.

"Looks like a safety deposit key." Michaella said.

"I don't remember this being here before. I guess I was too stunned about being adopted." JJ set the key and card aside and leafed through the pages to the ones her mother had written. Reading the one to her out loud, she came across the paragraph regarding the key.

> *"Honey, when you are old enough, I hope that you will find it in your heart to forgive me for what I did. It was the only way to protect you. If your father contacts you, please do not go with him. If at any point you search for me and can't locate me, he was probably the cause. Use what you find in this safety deposit box against him. I was able to get something on him that should put him away for life, that, and keep you safe. I truly loved you and thought this was the best way to protect you from the animal that he is. You are my heart. Love, your mother."*

JJ sat with the papers on her lap, not realizing that she was crying. She had never placed blame on her birthmother. And yes, after meeting her father, she knew why she had done it. She would do what she could to see to it that her mother's efforts didn't go unnoticed.

Chapter 26

Locking and leaving the moving van behind, they all got back into the truck. This time Paul got in the driver seat and Dennis co-piloting. Reed was going through the papers with the women in the back seat. Since it was late in the day, they went to the hotel were Michaella, Paul and Dennis stayed before, getting three rooms. With their luggage in their rooms, they went down to the restaurant for dinner.

During dinner they talked about the contents of the letters and the fact that the safety deposit box was actually in Detroit. They would need to have JJ with to access the box, so would fly there as two hundred and fifty miles was too far to drive and still be back to New York as soon as possible. Reed let Henry know of the plans to head to Detroit, then for the three men to head back to the big apple while Michaella and JJ flew back to Chicago. The men would take a commercial flight and the women would be taken back by Henry in the jet, from there they would drive Paul's truck to Michaella's house and stay there until this was over.

Dennis didn't like it, leaving them unprotected like that, but he wanted to make sure Giovanni was taken down. It was decided after a long, heated conversation for Reed to stay with the women and just Spook and Thumper would take the items back to Gage. Plans made, the bill paid for, they walked back up to their rooms and said good nights until morning where they would meet before heading back east.

Back in New York, Gage was in his room at his computer when the knock came at his door. He didn't even have to guess who it was, the Lattimers. Well, he also knew exactly how they would react to having the women taken out without their knowledge.

Opening the door, "Hi," was all he said as they walked in.

"Where in the hell are the others?" Nick said, at least he was pretty sure it was Nick. "We went by their rooms and the maids were cleaning them."

Gage took in the stern looks from both men before glancing down at his watch. It was late afternoon already and hearing from Henry, he knew the plane had already touched down north of Chicago.

"Chicago would be my guess." Gage said calmly.

This time it was Nate that spoke, trying not to explode, "Chicago? I thought we were going to wait until we had more men to get them out?"

Reaching for his coffee mug, Gage sized up the twins. He knew all about both of them. They worked together better than any other two people he knew; working almost as one person, they knew each other so well. He had done his own checks on their service time, where they had been stationed and under what commands. Their commendations were well earned. He had no doubts they were clean, but what of all of the people working with them.

"Spook didn't like that we were hit this morning, losing Marco. It came back to what JJ had asked, how did Giovanni know Marco was here? Spook wasn't taking any more chances on having JJ in any danger from her father, or anyone else for that matter. We worked quickly, quietly and without incident and got the women out of the city." To change the subject and let them stew over the mole aspect, he said, "They found a safety deposit key in with the letters."

The brothers looked at each other, curious about this new development.

"So, what was in the box?" Nick asked.

Swallowing his last bit of coffee, Gage reached for the carafe to refill his cup. "Don't know. The box is in a different city and they will get to take a look in the morning." He took a drink and realized the coffee had gone cold. He set it down and pushed it away, picking up his phone.

"Reed said they should be at the bank when it opens and hopes that JJ won't have any issue getting into the box. Then they will fly back here. Now, if you don't mind, I would like to call my wife, to check in and talk to my kids."

What could they do now but wait until morning? The twins gave Gage one more look before turning and leaving. Gage laughed and set the phone back down. He had already talked to Marlena and the kids after the others had left. A quiet supper in the restaurant downstairs should suffice before he went to bed.

Taking long learned precautions, Gage slipped his phone in his pocket along with the room key. Then he made sure that nothing was out of place before shutting down his computer and putting it in the room safe. Satisfied, he opened the door and went in search of a big steak.

The next morning JJ woke before Dennis. She wasn't used to sleeping with anyone and it made her more conscience about herself. She had slept better last night than she had in months, maybe years. There was such a connection between the two of them, it was too hard to explain, even to herself. The new intimacy made that bond even stronger. Smiling, she gently touched Dennis, feeling the strong muscle tone of his arms and back. His body was so much different from her own. She was petite, slim but toned. He was tall, almost bulky yet graceful in an athletic way.

And his eyes, she had never seen anyone with such pale colored eyes. They weren't really green and you couldn't call them blue either. They were so light in color, you could almost call them silver with streaks of light green and blue. Very unusual! She wondered if that was really how he had gotten his nickname.

JJ didn't know how long she laid touching and looking at the man next to her until he opened his eyes, smiled and swiftly rolled her beneath him.

"My turn!" was all he said in a voice raspy with sleep and lust. His internal clock told him they had plenty of time, so he took his time loving her. They had ample time for loving, showering and dressing, before they would meet the others to grab breakfast before leaving for the plane.

"You are so beautiful! You are also so mine!" Dennis made those declarations when he was finally able to speak after loving her. He rested his forehead on hers looking deeply, lovingly into her eyes.

JJ smiled back, not able to say the words that were really in her heart. She was pretty sure she was in love with him, but since she had never really had those feelings for anyone other than the Willis', wasn't exactly sure. The love she felt for the elder couple was more than what she had felt for her adoptive family.

He saw her struggle, watching her think and didn't need her to think about their relationship. He rolled over, got up and held his hand for her. Trustingly, she took it and they moved into the bathroom. He started the shower and stepped in. She took care of her other business and followed him in.

They met the others in the lobby for a quick, continental breakfast before heading to the airplane. Conversations revolved around the safety deposit box and what it might contain. Everyone speculated but only time would tell. They all went to the truck and rode over to meet Henry. Since Reed had let him know of their plans, he was fueled and ready for them. Once in the air, Dennis called Gage to find out what was going on in New York. They were brought up to date on the Lattimers and their reaction to the men taking the women out yesterday. Dennis wasn't surprised; they didn't seem like the type to be left out of the loop and wanted to be the ones in control of all situations. Gage hadn't seen or talked to them yet today, but was sure they would be at his door by mid-morning. They would touch bases again after the bank.

The bank was a small branch and JJ didn't have any trouble getting access to her box since it really was in her birth name and she had her original birth certificate and adoption papers. JJ didn't want to spend any more time than necessary there, so just took the large envelope, closed the box and met Dennis back in the lobby. They didn't waste any time and walked quickly to the rental, where the others waited.

Reed drove them to a small diner, somewhere they wouldn't be noticed and they took a large booth in the back. Ordering a light lunch, they waited until the waitress had brought their sandwiches before JJ broke the seal on the package. The items she dumped out shocked them all.

First was a thick copy of a ledger pages with names, dates and amounts on it. Next were video and audio cassettes, CDs, pictures, miscellaneous letters and another envelope to JJ from her mother. It was interesting that they would have to find old tech to view what was on tapes and to listen to what was recorded on the silver discs, but considering how long these items were in the box, it made sense.

Dennis flipped through the pictures and found they were mostly of JJ's father; one of him holding a gun while standing over someone with a big blood stain on his shirt. He had no idea how someone was able to get the picture and live but perhaps it was JJ's mother and she hadn't. They would have to get all of this to the Lattimers, who would be able to get it to all of the prosecutors in Giovanni's cases. This evidence was the key to locking the man away for a long time, as long as the information made it into the proper hands.

As they finished their lunch, Dennis put everything back in the package. He fished out enough money for their lunch and slid out of the booth. The others slid out too with the women heading to the restroom. Watching them walk away, Paul and Dennis liked the view. Reed just laughed and headed the opposite direction to the truck.

Chapter 27

As Reed, Michaella and JJ got off the jet back in Chicago, the women worried about Paul and Dennis. They had learned not to take anything for granted especially when it came to someone with a demented mind like JJ's father. There wasn't anything they could do, whether they wanted to or not. It was clear to both of them that the farther away they were, the better.

They thanked Henry and got in the truck. Reed would have them stop at the car rental place so he could get a vehicle. He would follow them, making sure that no one else did the same. When he slid behind the wheel of another truck, they all headed west to Michaella's house. Driving until almost dark, they found a little bed and breakfast for the night. Since the guys didn't want them to drive on the main roads, they had plotted a route that took them through little towns and communities.

JJ called Dennis after they had checked in and eaten. "Hi." It was all she could come up with saying to the man who had clearly become a significant part of her life. Not only did he come to help her, he was now her protector and lover.

"Hi back! How was your flight back to the windy city?" Dennis had walked out into the hall to talk to her. He closed his eyes to envision her, what she had been wearing, how she smelled.

"Uneventful. Henry was really nice. Reed rented a truck and is following us. We drove for several hours before finding a little B & B to stay the night." She was so relieved to hear his voice. "How was your flight?"

He could hear the nervousness in her voice. Man, he wished they were together "It was crowded. And loud. I haven't flown commercially for a long time. I guess I got spoiled flying in private planes. There must have been six crying kids on our plane alone. Then the walk through the airport to get our rental car had us bumping shoulders with more people. I can't image having to do that a lot."

JJ started to laugh at his telling of their flight. Dennis smiled to himself. It really wasn't that bad and he might have exaggerated a little bit, but it was great to hear her laugh.

"You should have seen the Lattimers' faces when we dropped that package on the table. You could almost see them salivate, it was almost gross. They called the city, state and federal DA's to set up a meeting. They were a little pissed we wouldn't let them have the original evidence though. Gage told them there was no way in hell we were letting it out of our sight until the meeting tomorrow." He looked up and down the hall, it was still clear. "They left but said one of them would be back to stay with us so the evidence would be protected. Thumper and Gage just laughed at them. Apparently, they didn't realize that they were dealing with three former SEALS."

She was still laughing when he asked softly what she was wearing. That stopped the delightful sound. He could almost hear her thinking on the other end of the phone. Now it was his turn to laugh.

"Don't tell me," he said. "Just let me imagine it until we are together again." Letting go with a few more chuckles he asked, "Are you enjoying your time alone with Michaella?"

This pleased her, that he would know what it meant to her. "Yes, the stress of the last few weeks are starting to fade and I can stop looking over my shoulder. We've talked and laughed and just been quiet. I have learned more about her in the last few hours than I had done over the years we have known each other. She talked about their wedding and your friends in Montana." She took a breath, wondering if she was boring him but continued on. "She showed me the pictures of the new baby and the big brother. They are so precious!"

Again, laughing he admitted, "That little girl is going to be so spoiled! As one of her uncles, I can say that I will love every minute of it. Liam is a handful and all boy. I can't wait for you to meet the whole family." He stopped before going on as someone passed him in the hall. "When this is all over, we'll take a trip to Montana for you to meet them. I think you will love them. You and Belinda are really a lot alike. Carrick can come off as an ogre but he loves his family and will do anything for them."

"Dennis, I would really like to meet your friends." She paused, thinking again. "Do you really think this will be over soon. That they will finally be able to get him and bring justice for my mother?"

Dennis could hear the hesitation in her voice. He knew she was still scared of her own father, or should he say monster. He would rather see the man dead instead of spending time in prison, but New York no longer had the death penalty. Now, if he had warrants in other states, like Florida, maybe there was a chance that the death penalty will be put back on the table. Those questions though were for the federal prosecutor. For now, all he could do was to reassure her with what he knew.

"JJ, the lawyers will do everything in their power to see that he is brought to justice. Maybe not the justice I would prefer, but according to the law of the land. Just know, we will do everything we can tomorrow to get all of your mother's evidence into the right hands and they'll be able to do their job to bring your father down."

Waiting for her response, his own gut and nerves started to get to him.

"JJ," Dennis said quietly, "are you still with me? Do you believe me, I will do anything to make sure you are safe from him?"

"Yes, I believe you." She whispered. "Dennis, I miss you."

That statement almost brought him to his knees. To know that they had only been apart for a few hours, and have her say something which would mean more to him than he couldn't begin to fathom.

"I miss you too, sweetheart!" Swallowing, he added, "We'll be together soon, I promise. Goodnight and JJ?"

He paused for her to reply. When she acknowledged him, he added, "Dream of me!" After hearing her light laugh, he hung up.

He stood there with his back up against the wall trying to bring himself back under control. Her trust in him, after all that she had been through was more than anyone not on his team had done. Sure, his family trusted him. All of his team members, past and present, trusted him. But he had never met a woman who first needed him and second gave him what JJ just did. He would make sure he didn't let her down.

Making his way back into the room, he caught Thumper telling Gage something about the items on the table. Thumper stopped mid-sentence.

"Spook, I think we should make copies of this and give them to the Lattimers. Evidence, witnesses and jurors seem to disappear when it has something to do with Giovanni. I don't think we should take that chance. I trust the Lattimers, but can we trust the lawyers?"

"I think you're right Thumper," Dennis said. "How long do you think we have before one of the twins return?"

Gage looked at his watch, "Well, they've been gone for about fifteen minutes. I don't know if we have half an hour or more. We might be able to get the papers and photos copied downstairs before they return. We can slip the CD's into my computer and try and copy to my hard drive, but there is no way we can copy the cassettes and VCR tapes before they get back."

Thumper took his phone out and called Geek, putting him on speaker. "Hey, Geek how's it going?" He waited, listening to their computer guru on the other end. When he stopped, he was asked, "Tell us what you know about the best way to copy some old VCR and cassette tapes?"

"Shit, are you kidding me? Who uses those anymore?" Geek exclaimed.

It was Gage who responded, "The person who did it died more than twenty-five years ago, that's who. We recovered evidence left to JJ from her mother, now can you help us or not?" Gage didn't take subordination well.

"Sorry Boss! Where are you, maybe I can get you some help." Geek said with a little more of a subdued attitude.

Thumper gave him the hotel name, address and room number. They knew he had someone close that could help them, the big question was would they have the ability to get here quickly.

"Okay," Geek said as he typed quickly. "I am sending a buddy to you, he is about ten minutes away. His name is Deuce." They heard more typing. "Can you get a couple VCR machines from the hotel, and maybe a cassette player?"

Dennis was already out the door and moving with purpose down the hall to the stairs. He could control his speed on the steps better than the unknown stops an elevator might make. If he needed to get more items, Thumper or Gage would let him know by text. He entered the lobby and headed toward the concierge's desk. He made his request and got the most amusing look. Art, the concierge, said to follow him. Fortunately, they still had a stash of old equipment in the basement, and he would love to get rid of some of it. Dennis was taken to the bowels of the hotel, where he found everything they would need. Art, trying to be very helpful, said they could have access to whatever was down there.

Dennis called up to Gage and ran over what he had found while Geek was still on the phone. As Geek listed all of the items needed, Dennis started stacking items on a nearby cart. He was actually lucky enough to find a box of new, unused VCR tapes in a box labeled for security. They must have gotten them, then switched over to digital recording equipment for the hotel. For good measure, Dennis rooted around a little more and also found some new cassettes. Just before he left, he spotted something else they could also use, so added it to the cart.

With everything on the cart, he pushed it over to the service elevator. A few short seconds later, he emerged on their floor and pushed the cart through the door of their room. He had barely time to unload any of it in one of the bedrooms before there was a light knock on the door. Gage looked out the peep hole to see a nerdy looking guy there. Opening the door, Deuce was a little surprised to see the three men there and all of the equipment.

It was a good thing they actually had a suite; it was big enough for Deuce to set up everything in one of the bedrooms, where they could close a door and keep it out of sight. Gage grabbed the small copier which Dennis found at the last minute and plugged it in and began copying the papers. Within a half hour, they were in the process of watching the first tape while it was being recorded. The scenes played out on it were like watching a 'B' rated Hollywood movie. The only difference was this was real, the people not actors and the results deadlier. There was no way Giovanni was going to wiggle out of this. The person filming it all knew what they were doing, there was no doubt about it.

They were on the second to last cassette when another knock came at the door. That had to be the Lattimers, or one of them, anyway. Gage took his time going to the door. Thumper and Spook were closed behind the door of the other room before Gage opened it to let one of the twins enter.

Gage wasn't taking any chances, and glanced down the hall before he closed and bolted the door. As he turned to look at the man who had just entered, believing it to be Nate, knew something was wrong.

"Spill it Nate! What's wrong?"

Nate was, first, surprised that Gage knew which of the twins had come to the room and second, knew something was wrong. Now, he had no choice to tell the three men here what he himself had just found out.

"We've lost our eyes on Giovanni. Our surveillance man was

159

found dead and stuffed in a garbage dumpster. We won't know for a little while yet how long ago he had been killed. Nick is doing all he can to find out more and get a better assessment of when Giovanni slipped out of his safe house."

Spook and Thumper had come back into the room during the explanation. Spook was about to leave the room when Thumper grabbed him, holding him back until they knew more.

"So, has he left his house to go somewhere else, or to see Watters? Did he know about Caruso taking JJ?" Spook was almost spitting his words at Nate.

Nate turned to answer him, "We really don't know yet. Nick is checking the tracers we had on most of his cars and our internal informant has gone silent."

It was Gage's turn to ask some questions, "Do you still have eyes on Watters and Caruso?"

"Yes, they haven't moved or gone anywhere, as far as we can tell. No phone calls in or out of either location." Nate could see his news wasn't good for any of them.

Spook started to pace around the room. Stopping at the dark window, he turned back to ask Nate, "Who knew about this new evidence?"

Nate was finally beginning to believe there was a mole in the system. The brothers had called the state district attorney, and told him that they had new evidence which, would mean a whole new round of charges against the notorious head of the Giovanni syndicate. The state DA was going to call the city and federal DA's with the news and set the meeting in the morning. The meeting had been set for one in the afternoon, giving all parties time to get to the courthouse to view the new materials JJ found.

"Well, it's a damn good thing that we got JJ and Michaella out of the city and on their way to a safe place." Thumper said. He knew he felt better about it, but Spook was the one he was worried about. He could raise a hell of a lot of havoc and there were some that wouldn't know what hit them.

Maybe it was time to actually show Nate what they had and what they were doing in the other room. Perhaps he might be able to get a handle on how to go about finding the mole, and slipping the noose more securely around the neck of one Giovanni.

The door to the other room opened and took away any questions about whether to let Nate in on any of what was going on it there. Deuce stopped in his tracks, looking at the new man in the room.

"I think you better come and take a look at this." It was all Deuce had to say before returning to the other room. Having enough equipment to do so, Deuce had three TVs playing at the same time, watching the footage and recording it at the same time.

On one screen, Giovanni was waving both hands at a woman, clearly JJ's mother, a gun in his right hand. Seconds later, he wasn't waving either hand but holding the gun pointed directly at the woman. In the background, you could see the infant standing in a crib; an infant in pink clothing. The sound was garbled, but the indication was clear: Giovanni was threatening the woman. She dropped to her knees, begging him. He stopped pointing the weapon at her and set it on the end table, before picking up a glass with an amber liquid in it.

The second screen showed Giovanni talking with a young man dressed in a suit. It wasn't hard to see Marco in the face of the young man. That wasn't the shocker though. It was the fact that even though the room was the same, the crib was now gone. Like this video was taken after JJ and her mother were gone.

"Deuce, is there any way to tell when these were recorded?" Gage asked.

"I will have to do some scrubbing on them, I can't really say for sure though." His attention was on the third screen.

The other men turned to see the sitting state DA, Gilbert, in a room with Giovanni having drinks. This view was from a different room altogether, but it was obvious that the men were more than friends. Again, sound would have been nice, to hear the conversation. Well, this explained more than anything else. Here was their mole! Here was the reason Giovanni had gotten away with so much. He had a clear inside track to the judicial system in the state.

Nate had gone completely still! He had been working with the man on the screen for nearly a year, at the DA's request to the FBI, to get enough evidence to put Giovanni away. Nate had actually liked the Gilbert. He took a few steps back, bumping into the bed, sitting down with a perplexed look.

"Fuck," Nate spat out. "That bastard!" Nate then realized what was going on in the room. "You're actually dubbing the tapes!"

Standing back up, he walked to the table where the copy machine was sitting and the duplicate and original papers sitting in two stacks beside it. Picking up one stack, he looked toward Gage.

Gage answered without knowing the question, "You, yourself said that Giovanni was a slippery bastard. Evidence, witnesses and jurors disappeared. We were just making sure that this damning evidence didn't have the same results." He stepped up to Nate, "Is there any way to push this meeting up, without the state DA? Perhaps with only the federal DA?"

Nate took out his phone, but before he could make the call, Gage stopped him by adding, "Maybe we should watch all of the footage first? We don't want any other surprises or what else might be on the tapes."

Nate agreed but thought they may need one more set of eyes. He called his brother, telling him to bring coffee and carbs, they would need it.

With stale coffee odor in the rooms, the men had stayed up all night reading all of the print material, watching all of the video and listening to all of the other recordings. Deuce had slipped out only long enough to go grab some of his other computer equipment to scrub the tapes enough to hear what was being said. By morning, they had all they needed for a case against the Gilbert, some of his staff along with quite a few other city officials.

By piecing all of the information together, there was no way that JJ's mother had put all of it in the safety deposit box. She had someone else who knew about what she was doing and had access to the box. Gage's guess was that it had been Marco, from the conversations they had on the plane and after, before they found JJ, Marco was more than JJ's guardian angel. All that mattered now, was how they could use it in the most effective manner.

Chapter 28

By noon, Spook was fit to be tied with frustration. They still had no idea what happened to Giovanni. Watters was making waves about not getting his virgin bride. Somehow, he had found out that Caruso had abducted her and planned on ransoming her off to get a bigger slice of the pie. Watters didn't take kindly to that and put a hit out on Caruso. Since then, the feds had him and the four men who took JJ in custody, Watters was taking his anger out on Giovanni's men. From what they could tell, Giovanni was already down six men, eight if you count the two the Lattimers took out when they came after Marco.

Since Geek still had federal access, he was combing security video on the streets, bus and train stations, as well as the airlines for any glimpse of Giovanni. It was like the man had completely vanished off the face of the earth. They were tapping all of their resources to find the man, to no avail.

Nate had been able to reschedule the meeting with Gilbert on the pretense there was a delay on getting the holder of the evidence into the meeting with adequate protection. They had until four that afternoon to do what needed to be done. Meanwhile, they had contacted the federal attorney and met with him in private up in the suite to show him the incriminating videos against state DA Gilbert. Hankinson, the federal DA was too astonished to say much. He kept looking at the screen, then the Lattimers and then to Gage, Spook and Thumper. He asked a lot of questions to the validity of the information. Spook relayed as much a possible about JJ, her mother and Marco. Hankinson, got on the phone to a federal judge to get arrest warrants for Gilbert, his underlings, the city officials and Giovanni of course.

Hankinson would take the originals of the evidence, leaving the copies with the Lattimers for safe keeping. He instructed them to find a safe place to tuck them away until all of the trials were placed on the federal docket. He also asked about JJ and her whereabouts. Dennis was reluctant to divulge that information, saying that the fewer people who knew where she was, the better. Hankinson thought this over before totally agreeing with Dennis.

Getting ready to leave, Hankinson was stopped by Gage as he answered a call from Geek. He put the call on speaker to save time in relaying his information.

"Hey, Geek what have you got?"

There was a small hesitation before he spoke, "You aren't going to like this Gage, and Spook is going to like it even less."

"Spill it Geek." Spook said with all the pent-up frustration he was holding on to.

"I was finally able to locate Giovanni. I have him first on a security camera outside of LaGuardia Airport, getting out of a limo. I flipped over to the cameras within the airport and watched him go to the private charter plane concourse. With your permission, I will tap in and see what flight he has booked and to where."

Gage looked at Hankinson. He had known about Geek, actually used him for several of his more delicate cases.

"Geek, this is Hankinson. Go for it! I want to know where that bastard is headed, so he can be arrested."

"Yes sir." It was all Geek needed. They could hear keys being tapped as Geek worked quickly to find out answers. "Son of a bitch."

"Geek?"

"Sorry sir, I didn't mean to say that out loud. Thumper, you there?"

"Yep"

"Grab Spook! Giovanni is booked for Chicago. Isn't that where JJ was headed?"

It was a good thing he was given notice, Thumper did grab Spook and tried to contain him once he heard Giovanni was going after JJ. If anyone knew Spook better than he did, it was their team. They had a long-standing relationship, more family than others of the same blood.

"Damn it, let me go!" Spook shouted. "I have to call JJ and let her know." To his surprise, Thumper loosened his grip but didn't let go.

"Spook, you can't go off halfcocked." Gage said softly, in his authoritative voice. "Cool your jets and Thumper will let you go."

When Thumper felt the tight muscles relax, he let his best friend go. "We cool?"

Taking a cleansing breath, Spook knuckle pumped his best friend. "We're cool, now can I call her?"

Nodding, Gage walked away with Hankinson to the other room, so Spook and Thumper could make the call. It had only been a few hours since they had talked. Michaella had called them once they were on the road around eight this morning, in that time they were nearly home to Michaella's house.

"JJ, how are you?" Dennis couldn't help the waver in his voice. He waited apprehensively for her reply.

"We're good. We just picked up groceries and Michaella said we should be at the house in twenty minutes or so. What's up?"

"Damn, you girls made good time." Wanting to lighten the bad news, he joked with them. "Can you pull over and stop? We have bad news."

Both men waited until Michaella said that they were stopped. After they had stopped, Reed walked up to the truck and they rolled down the window so he could hear.

"You know we went through all of the evidence last night and were meeting with the DA today. Well, the state DA is in bed with Giovanni. Warrants have been issued for both men, Gilbert was

166

apprehended, but Giovanni disappeared sometime late yesterday. This morning, Geek spotted him getting on a private plane to Chicago. Our thoughts are he is coming to find you, JJ. How he knew you were headed back there, we don't know." Dennis took a second to put his thoughts in order before continuing.

"Who is driving?" he asked.

Michaella answered, "I am. Since we were going to my house, I know the back way."

"Okay. First go to the back seat of the truck and lift up on the bench. Under it, you should find two hand guns and ammo. There is also a shot gun, but leave that there for now. Second, go to Thumper's," he paused, "or better yet, my place. It's deeper in the woods, which makes it harder to find and get to. Mic you know the code for Thumper's house and have the key."

Thumper jumped in, "Michaella, love, I have a key to Spook's house and I really think you should go there until we can get there. It is more concealed, the road sucks and it's less traveled. Do you remember where I put my gun in the bathroom closet?"

"Yes."

"Good, if you go to the same lock box you will find a key. It is for Spook's door."

"Okay, Dennis do you have an alarm system like Paul's?"

"Well," Dennis chuckled, "Mine is more complex, but basically they are the same. The code is two sets of numbers, got a pen?"

They could hear the women talking about pens, paper and the guns. "Okay," Michaella said, "JJ is ready to write the codes while Reed is getting the guns."

Not realizing it, Dennis nodded. "JJ the first set of numbers is six digits: 060199. After you enter these, press the green button once and immediately enter these next six digits: 092182. After the second set, hit the green button twice. That will disengage the security. Once you are settled back in the house, reverse the code numbers only. Understand?"

JJ was quiet for a few seconds before responding. "Got it! To get in 060199 green button once, then 092182 and green button twice. To reset, 092182 green button once and 060199 green button twice."

"That's correct." Spook was happy JJ was a quick learner. Added to the fact that she had great instincts would ease his mind a little.

"Maybe it would be better if you left the truck at my house and used the path up to Spook's." Thumper was thinking out loud. "Michaella, do you think you can find the path up?"

Dennis picked up on his line of thought. If Giovanni had been able to find out where they were headed, he would need a tracker to find the smaller cabin tucked back in the trees and brush.

"That's a really good idea. Michaella, do you think you will be able to get all of your things up there?" he asked.

Michaella had taken both guns and the full clips for them from Reed. "I guess so. There is the backpack I left there and I can probably find a second one. We can leave the majority of JJ's stuff in the back of the truck, just take some clothes and food up."

Reed had another thought, "We can head over to Michaella's, leaving your truck in her garage and drive the rental up to Thumper's. Since I am here, I'll get the girls settled at Spook's. I can stay at Thumper's. That way, I'll be close by in case I'm needed.

Dennis knew he had plenty of rations; winters got long in the woods. "Mic, there should be plenty of wood cut, and there is an abundance of home canned goods, dried fruits and veggies. The freezer is full too. Take as little as possible and get into hiding." He didn't mean to come off as sounding gruff, he was just worried for their safety.

"Michaella, Spook didn't mean to sound like a drill sergeant. We're just worried about you getting hidden as soon as possible. With Reed close, it helps. We'll be there as soon as possible. Love you!"

"Oh, one more thing." Dennis said quietly. "Check your cell phones once you are up there. If they aren't getting full reception, there is a sat phone in a metal box under the bed. Pull it out and check the power on it. Make sure it is fully charged. If we can't reach you on your cells, we'll call the sat."

"Oh, hey," Paul interrupted, "I have a sat phone too. It's in the same closet Mic." He paused to consider them alone in the woods and whether anything was forgotten. "Any questions?" Thumper inquired. It wasn't like they had the time to go over a check list.

Dennis took one last breath to say, "JJ, follow your instincts. If something feels off, like it did the other day, go with your feelings first. Call Reed first then us. If it's possible, we'll get help to you as soon as possible." Spook had changed the tone of his voice. It was important that JJ knew he had confidence in her. "And JJ, I love you!"

Good-byes were said and they hung up. Now to head east. Spook and Dennis were already packing their meager items when the other men came back into the room.

"Airport security missed Giovanni, and the tower wasn't able to keep the plane on the ground." Nick said as he had come into the suite, holding his phone in his hand.

Gage knew the flight times and they only had a few hours before Giovanni got to Chicago. He took his phone out and was about to call Henry when Hankinson told the Lattimers to use the FBI jet, it would be faster and large enough for all of them. It was a good thing too, as Henry would have had to flown from Chicago to get them and then fly back, wasting valuable time.

Nate was on the phone lining up the plane as the others bundled up the copies of the evidence. Putting the duplicates into one box, it was decided to overnight the copies to Gage's ranch. He would call Marlena and instruct her to have one of their hands take the box to the mountain cabin. The box would be well out of reach for anyone to find; even if they had any inkling to look for them in Montana, someone would have to have enough mountain knowledge to get to the cabin, alone. When the room was clear of their personal effects, they all walked out, not looking back.

Chapter 29

With Dennis's truck stored and locked in Michaella's garage, they checked the house quickly and everything was as they had left it before heading to Montana several weeks ago. JJ fell in love with the quaint little town and thought it was a lot like where she grew up, only smaller. She decided maybe she was due for a change and figured this would be a good place as any, as long as Dennis, Michaella and Paul were close by.

The weather was taking a drastic change and it looked as though it would be snowing soon. Reed slid behind the wheel as Michaella took the front passenger seat. JJ was more comfortable in the back since she was the smallest. They had to reload everything to the truck Reed rented, with the items they didn't want wet in the cab and the rest in the back. With a quick look at Michaella then JJ, Reed set off for Thumper's place.

JJ couldn't help watching as the scenery went by. The community was small and quaint, but everyone moved with a distinct purpose. There were small, charming specialty shops, coffee cafes and eateries. She even saw the local library in its statuesque, old brink building. They drove by a closed drive-in before heading completely out of town.

After ten, or maybe it was even fifteen minutes, Reed veered off and taking a left on what looked like a less traveled road. The fall colors here must be beautiful, JJ thought as she looked out to the mostly barren trees. There were only a few that still had their leaves, which were a burnt orange in color. Those few trees dotted the hillside and across the river she could now see below them. It surprised her when Reed turned off the road once again and drove further into the woods. A short time later, he stopped in front of a cabin about the same size as Michaella's house in town. Behind it there was a garage or shop.

Michaella hopped out of the truck and headed up the deck to the door, keys in her hand. After the door swung open and alarm disengaged, she turned and smiled back to Reed and JJ.

"Welcome to our home, JJ!"

JJ took the steps up to the opened door, stopped and gave Michaella a hug, then whispered, "Thank you!"

"You don't need to thank me, we're friends! Friends help each other." Michaella smiled, then motioned for JJ to enter the cabin. "Make yourself at home while I change clothes, pack and find the items we will need before heading up to Dennis's. Would you want to help Reed bring in our stuff? We can sort through it in the kitchen and decide how much we can actually carry up the trail on foot."

After a quick look around, JJ found a nice size kitchen and dining area with an open view to the living room where there was a big fireplace. It was almost too quiet here, but not in an uncomfortable way. As she gazed at the fireplace, she could imagine Michaella and Paul snuggled in front with a glass of wine or hot chocolate. She shook the image away and turned back to help Reed.

She mentally went through her available clothes as they hauled stuff in. JJ would have to pull out something more durable and warmer for their trek to Dennis's place. She knew she didn't have a warmer coat, wondering if Michaella had something that would fit her. After they had all of the boxes in, she opened her suitcase and picked out jeans, sweaters, socks and long sleeve shirts. With the pile of clothes on the floor, she selected a warm outfit and stepped into the bathroom and changed.

Coming out with her travel clothes tucked under her arm, JJ smiled at Michaella and stepped up to her hodge podge of items. She would have to figure out a way to get what was necessary in the backpack that Michaella laid out for her. Just stuffing them in wouldn't work, so she carefully rolled each item and nestled them in the bag. Once done, it was clear she would still have room for her cosmetic bag and perhaps a few other smaller items.

Reed had put food items in his bag until it was full, while Michaella did the same with her own clothes. They talked casually about the walk up to Dennis's, and decided that once there, Reed could take one of the empty packs and come back down for more of the girls' clothing items. Reed would keep Paul's satellite phone, so they would be able to communicate between the two cabins. He didn't want to guess how long it would take for Spook and Thumper to get to them, or whether they would be going after Giovanni himself.

They each picked up their packs and walked out onto the deck while Michaella locked up the house. Reed had already pulled the truck into the garage upon Michaella's urging. Taking the lead, Michaella picked her way through the trees on an unseen trail, up a slight incline. It wasn't a worn path, as far as JJ could tell. Actually, she couldn't even fathom how Michaella knew which way to go; they zig zagged up to trees or boulders then moved around or over the obstacles.

Minutes later, a cabin appeared out of nowhere and they were standing in a small clearing. Walking up to the door, JJ pulled the code out of her pocket as Michaella took the key she located at Paul's and opened the door. As quickly as possible, JJ entered the codes Dennis had given her and then saw the disengaged signal show in the little window of the security pad.

JJ set her bag down and looked around the small kitchen they were standing in. It was functional, but no way near as big as the one Paul had or even Michaella's in town. Through the short hallway she spied a living area with a fireplace and a large chair. There were a few other doors, which she figured were bedrooms and a bathroom.

They took care of the groceries they brought up before looking for the box with the sat phone and its charger. As Dennis has suspected, their cell phones had very little reception. The sat phone had a slight charge but they wanted it completely charged, so set it up on the kitchen counter.

Reed made sure they felt settled and safe before heading back down the hill to Thumper's. Michaella gave him the keys and the code for Thumpers system. Since it was getting darker by the minute, Michaella didn't want Reed to try and come back up tonight. He argued with her, but in the end, she won and he would come back in the morning. She laughed and said she would have the coffee ready when he got back. They started to see the snowflakes come down, looking pretty like a postcard as they said their good-byes as he stood on the deck. The sun was already down below the hill line as he disappeared down the hill. The women grabbed some more wood for the fire before heading inside and locking the door and securing the system for the night. It was clear they would have a deep coverage in the morning by the looks of the increasing large, white flakes.

With the fire blazing, wine and sandwiches on the little coffee table, JJ and Michaella sat listening to the night wind through the empty trees. Sitting for a long time without talking, they both seemed to be deep in thought; wondering where the men were, what Giovanni was up to and if they would actually be safe here in the woods.

JJ was sure she was safe for now; there was no way a city man like her father would find her in this place without having a guide to bring him to it. Before they locked themselves in, she had taken a few quick glances around and she couldn't see a road let alone any other houses or cabins. You couldn't even see Paul's place from here.

"JJ, are you alright?" Michaella asked quietly.

JJ looked up from her clasped hands and to her dearest friend. "Yes. How about you?"

Smiling, Michaella took a drink from her wine glass. "I'm tired but feeling good. You don't need to worry, we should be really safe here. Paul and Dennis wouldn't have sent us here if they didn't think we would be."

"I know, I trust Dennis and Paul. I just wonder what Giovanni is up to." JJ took a drink and reached for a sandwich. "Do you think they will be able to find him and get him in jail?"

"We have to believe they will. I think with the evidence you got, the federal DA has more than enough to put Giovanni away for a long time. I got the impression the Lattimers are standup guys, like Paul, Dennis, Gage and Reed. They didn't come off as letting this go just because the man slipped away." Michaella reached for a sandwich. "They're cut from the same cloth as our guys. Justice and doing what's right is in their blood."

JJ knew her friend was right! Just because Giovanni had gotten away this time, didn't mean they would give up, not now they had the information her mother died to protect. She thought then of Marco. If he was the other person who knew about the box, why hadn't he done more to help her find it? Was it the fact that she had pretended not to know she was adopted and didn't know about her real parents? JJ guessed she would never know. It was just sad Marco had to die before getting himself out. One more strike against her father.

After several hours of small talk, more wine and canned fruit they had found, both women headed to bedrooms. The first door opened was undoubtedly a guest room. Michaella said she would take it and let JJ have the other room. Saying good night, Michaella set her bag on the bed and closed the door.

JJ stepped up to the door they had left open. She could almost feel Dennis in the space of his bedroom. The bed was large and made with a homemade quilt on top. There was only one chest of drawers, a night stand with a lamp and what she supposed was a closet door. She had left the box out from under the bed.

Carefully, she looked through it and found more than the phone had been in the box. It was filled with items from his military days; a deadly looking knife, what looked like goggles, gloves, dark clothes and many more miscellaneous items. She found a picture of a group of men. It was easy to pick out Paul, Dennis, Gage and Reed. There were a few other men all posing for the camera. You could see the comradery with all of the men. This must be his unit when he served in the military. They were obviously a tight knit group. JJ put everything back the way she found it, closed the box and shoved it back under the bed.

Sitting on the bed, she removed her shoes and sweater. JJ took her few things out of the bag she had packed and realized she didn't have anything to sleep in. With a shrug of her shoulders, she opened one of the drawers of his dresser and found a soft T-shirt and a pair of jogging shorts she believed would work. After putting them on, JJ slid under the quilt and rested her head on the pillow. She was immediately aware of Dennis's scent on the pillow, in the sheets. Taking a deep breath, she closed her eyes to sleep; she was comforted by the smell of him, even though he was hundreds of miles away.

Chapter 30

Driving with an accelerated purpose, the Lattimers were trying to get them to the airport heading west as fast as possible. Hankinson cleared the way with the local law enforcement, before placing a call to airport security. Then he was on the phone to the Chicago FBI office, making sure there would be eyes on Giovanni when his plane landed. The Chicago agents were instructed to apprehend him, if at all possible, without any civilian interference. Too many people had been hurt already by that man, Hankinson didn't want any more in the loss column when it came to Giovanni.

When they reached the airport, as expected, the FBI pilot met them on the concourse where a sleek, dark colored jet sat. The copilot was at the top of the boarding stairs, waiting for the passengers to come up and be seated. Gage, shifting his bag to his left hand, headed over and took the offered hand from the pilot, before bounding up the steps. The Lattimers followed with their bags slung over their shoulders. Paul gave Dennis a look and quick punch to his shoulder just before taking the steps two at a time.

Since they weren't sure how this would go or what they may find when they got to Chicago, they all had their firearms on them, albeit concealed. With the word of Hankinson, they wouldn't have to worry about being stopped by any security. They all still had their military credentials, along with their security company's, which gave them the right to carry a concealed weapon, it was a good bet they wouldn't even catch the attention of anyone.

They all took a seat, separate from each other, so they wouldn't be tempted to talk. What they needed was some rest, and the two hours air time would give them some time to shut down and refresh. Dennis was edgy and was sure he wouldn't sleep, but knew his military training would kick in. He wouldn't do JJ any good if he was too tired to think clearly. His instincts were good, really good, but to be on the top of his game, he needed to be well rested and coherent.

Closing his eyes, Dennis concentrated on JJ. What she was doing, what she thought of his home, how she slept in his bed? Smiling to himself, he pictured her in his room, filling it with her special scent.

His place was small; he built it with only himself in mind. Buying the small parcel to be close to Thumper, his best friend, wasn't just by chance. They had been friends a long time and it seemed like a good idea at the time to live close to each other. Now, he needed to think about his connection with JJ and whether they could build their relationship into something more permanent. There was no way he was going to let her go, of that he was positive! He could easily add on to his cabin and make it more accommodating for her, if she was open to the idea. If not, he would go to wherever she was. It was his final thought as he tumbled into sleep.

Landing at the same airport as Giovanni had, they were just several hours later. The Chicago authorities hadn't been able to arrest him. He had a private limo waiting, so he had only to take a few steps from the plane to the waiting car. The first agents assigned to him had no choice but to follow him and know where he was going.

Dennis, Paul, Gage and the Lattimers climbed into a couple of cars along with two different agents and were taken to the same five-star hotel Giovanni had checked into. At the suggestion of the Lattimers, half of them would stay there and the others across the street. Dennis wanted to keep closer tabs on Giovanni, to know exactly what he was up to and how he had known to come back to Chicago, where JJ had worked and lived.

As they were about to get out of the car, Giovanni came out of the hotel front door, heading to a waiting car. As his car pulled out from the curb, they trailed behind. Since there was no way he would know he was being followed, they didn't worry about being too close. As it was, with the traffic and the time of day, it wasn't hard to keep a constant eye on the limo. The limo pulled up to a classy restaurant, where Giovanni got out and it took off. The car with Dennis, followed suit, dropping him off.

Dennis casually stepped up behind JJ's father to listen to the conversation Giovanni carried on with the maître d. With no reservation and his ample cash wasn't working to get a table, Giovanni took his cell out of his pocket to call for his car. Being prepared, Dennis carefully took the chance on a tracker, slipping it in Giovanni's coat pocket. It was only short range, so it would do for their purposes. It wouldn't help them if or when he changed his coat but it was all they had. As he forced himself to move away, Dennis controlled the desire to either draw his gun or raise his fists. He didn't have back up so had to leave. Dennis strode out the door, turned his phone on and checked for the tag to show on the screen. It was working, so he called Nate and informed him. They weren't too far away, so turned around and came back to get him.

Sliding back into the car, they waited for Giovanni's limo to return. They watched as he angrily stomped out and got in the back. Driving up to the next high-end restaurant, again the man walked into the building. They waited but he didn't come back out, so must have been seated to dine.

Nate, Dennis and Thumper stayed there waiting for Giovanni to eat, while Gage and Nick took at chance at getting into Giovanni's hotel room. Gage called Geek to get the exact room number and a way to get in unnoticed.

Back at the hotel, the men carefully went through the room and found nothing! He was registered, but had he actually come up to the room? There wasn't a suit case or hanging bag with any apparel whatsoever. There wasn't a shave kit in the bathroom. There was absolutely nothing to indicate the man had even entered the room.

They slipped listening devices and small cameras around the rooms then left it as they had found it.

Having the New York state and federal arrest warrants in hand, the federal agents said they wanted to wait until Giovanni was on the street. Dennis started to wonder if those agents were clean or dirty. Since Gage had sent a text that Giovanni's room was clean, not even a bag was there, was it just a front? Had he known they were coming for him? Or was he really traveling that light? He texted Geek to check the security cams from the airport, just to make sure the local agents were telling the truth about watching him get off the plane, with luggage. If so, where was it? Still riding around in the limo? This whole situation was starting to smell, Dennis thought. He sent his concern to Gage to contact Hankinson to have the agents checked out here. It was possible Giovanni had a long reach considering he seemed to know JJ was in Chicago for the last few years.

Chapter 31

JJ woke early the next morning with a start and chill; first not knowing where she was and second at how cold the room had gotten. The sun hadn't come up yet, as it was still pretty dark out. Taking the top quilt with her, she slid out of bed, dancing on the ice-cold floor to the window. She was amazed to see the snow was still falling, and how much had accumulated over the night. It had been a long time since she had seen that much pure, white, beautiful snow. With awe and wonder, she stood at the window and watched it fall, like small pillows of down falling. Smiling to herself, but sad too, wishing Dennis was here to watch the scenery change with her.

Taking a moment, she grasped now, with all that had been going on, how late it was in the year. Without realizing it, she had actually missed some of her favorite fall season's activities. The colors as the leaves changed, then dropped from the trees. The decorations at Halloween time, along with costumes and trick or treaters. JJ grabbed her phone to check the actual date. Had they actually missed Thanksgiving? No, it was next week. Then on to the Christmas season. Looking back outside, she wondered if this year could be as memorable as the year when Dennis had stayed with her family. Only time would tell.

Shifting over to her suitcase, she picked out warm clothes and quickly dashed across the hall to the bathroom. Turning on the shower to let the water warm, she took care of her other necessity. Stripping down, JJ stepped into the steaming cascade of water. Shampooing and washing as quickly as possible, she finished her shower in record time. She wanted to make sure there was hot water for Michaella to shower too. Dressing, combing her hair and applying some face lotion was all the prep she would do for now. They weren't going anywhere today, so to make herself any more presentable wasn't required. After running a quick toothbrush over her teeth, she straightened up the small bathroom and went to see about heating the cabin and making some coffee.

Noticing the fire still had some glowing coals, JJ added wood to the pile of embers in the fireplace. It wasn't long before the dry wood was engulfed in flames and the room started to heat up. Mesmerized by the flames, JJ took a few brief moments to dream what it would be like to live in such a rustic cabin with Dennis. She had always had just the basics around her; small apartments, easy furniture to upkeep, a small number of personal items. Only her last apartment was the most lavish she ever had, since leaving home some many years ago. Shaking her head, she knew she would have to wait until this business with her father was over before she could make any future plans.

Taking herself back to her initial task of coffee, she found all of the food supplies Dennis had mentioned last night. Touching one of the jars, JJ smiled to herself, remembering how Mrs. Willis always canned preserves, vegetables and the like every fall. She would often find her favorite pears in the tree house. By the looks of it, someone, probably his mother, really liked to garden and put items away for a snowy day. She took one of the jars to the counter for their breakfast.

Finding the coffee and filters, she went about starting the coffee maker before gathering more supplies for making a hearty meal for three. JJ was sure Reed would be along as soon as the sun was completely up, hoping the snow wouldn't hamper his trip to the cabin this morning. She heard Michaella moving on the other end of the house. Removing a slab of bacon from the freezer, it was much too firm to work with today, so she would thaw it for tomorrow. Grabbing a tube of country sausage and spying some frozen biscuits, knew a thick, creamy gravy with the sausage and biscuits would be a good start for a cold day.

Michaella came in as JJ finished browning the sausage in a large cast iron pan. Seeing the smile on JJ's face, Michaella couldn't help but comment. "Looks like someone is having fun in the kitchen this morning." Taking the offered mug of hot coffee, she took a chair at the small table.

"I was up early and was taken with the snow falling. I knew Reed would be hungry when he got here too." JJ picked up the jar of pears, "Look what I found! These will lighten up the meal and give us a sweet note to it too!"

Michaella couldn't hold back her smile. This was a different JJ from the one she saw only a few weeks ago. It was clear now how stressed and alone she must have been. Even Marco's quick death only a few days ago, seemed to have left her friend. There was no way she would do anything or say anything to bring those shadows back to JJ. An idea came to her mind to stay clear of all of the current drama.

"JJ, since leaving my ex behind, I have been thinking about starting a company of my own and wondering if you would like to join me as a partner." Michaella saw the hesitation come into JJ eyes. "Don't worry, I'm not asking for a financial commitment."

Taking out a bowl and the flour, JJ was relieved since she didn't want to start dipping into her funds really heavily right now. She started to make a roux for the white sauce.

"What I'm suggesting is for us to work together, from here of course. I am not really interested in going back to be in a big city. Since I travel a lot, consulting and so forth, maybe I or should I say we, could expand and use your organization skills and incorporate them into the consulting business." Michaella took a drink of her cooling coffee. "It's just an idea! But please, think about it."

This was something to think about! First, she needed to close the chapter involving her father. Then there was the new relationship with Dennis. She did like the thought of working with her only friend.

"I like the idea, Michaella! I'm flattered you would want me to be a partner. I will think about it seriously, but until this other drama is over, I can't give you a definite answer."

"That's all I can ask, JJ. I think we would make a great team!"

They heard something outside and stopped their conversation to peek out the window. It was Reed! He found the shovel and was clearing the small back deck so they could open the door and get to the wood pile. JJ disengaged the alarm and opened the door.

Smiling, JJ said, "Just in time! Coffee is ready and breakfast is nearly done."

Reed shook off the snow, stomped off his boots and shed his jacket. Slipping onto a chair, he took the mug of coffee Michaella handed him.

They talked casually about odd things, before they moved on to talking about whether anyone had heard from Paul or Dennis. Since they hadn't, Michaella asked about whether they should call them. Reed made the decision to keep quiet so they were still hidden. Silence was the best way to do that. They ate breakfast, hauled in more wood and started a pot of soup for later in the day. Michaella found a deck of cards and cribbage board to whittle away the time.

Back in Chicago, Gage was watching the door of Giovanni's hotel and swore under his breath before slowly getting up and telling Spook to come with him. They had decided to have coffee in the little shop off the lobby, keeping an eye on the door in case Giovanni came down. He was shocked to see who walked down with the crime boss, but none other than a man Gage had court martialed twenty years ago. The man had been a disgrace to the uniform, to say the least and his time in Leavenworth was a testament at his guilt. Being recognized right now would not help them out.

As they stepped away, Gage kept his back to the room and quietly asked Spook to look at the man in question. "Spook, see the man with the military haircut, brown shirt and pants that came down with Giovanni?"

"Yes, what's up?"

"Jones was under me in the unit about twenty some years ago, purely a bad seed. After his court martial, I occasionally kept tabs on him. What I learned was he is a bounty hunter or gun for hire. Can you shadow him and see what these two are doing together?"

Spook shot up a brow because it was silly to ask if he could shadow unseen. That was laughable! With nothing more than a nod, he slipped out of the café, around the corner and out into the street through a side door. It was not early by any means, there was enough foot traffic to make hiding in plain sight easy enough.

The two men stood talking on the side of the street as he stepped around the corner, and only did so briefly before Jones walked off and Giovanni went back inside. Jones looked around then moved on, walking at a brisk pace toward the north. He went on for several blocks before crossing the street and hailing a cab. Being a safe pace behind, Spook also hailed a cab asking the driver, former military by the looks of it, to follow at a safe distance of a car length or two.

Dennis carried on a casual conversation while they drove several cars back. He didn't really divulge anything crucial about himself or his reason for following the other cab. He found out the driver, Peterson, had been on tours in some of the same countries Dennis had been in and around the same time. Having the military background made it easy for them to talk, Dennis handed over one of his cards and said that if he ever wanted to look at the possibility of a position in security, to call.

His driver stopped at the same time the other cab did, only a half a block back. Jones got out of the cab, looked up and down the street before entering an electronics store. Dennis asked Peterson to wait and they would see how long he was in the store. After only ten, maybe fifteen minutes, Jones came out, stuffing a hand-held unit into his coat pocket. There was no way to know what it was without seeing it up close. Jones walked to the next corner, crossing the street to the run-down hotel on the corner.

Dennis took out his phone to call Gage. They had decided that Spook would stay where he was watching Jones, while Gage and the others kept tabs on Giovanni. Gage would have Geek find out all he could on Jones and the store he came out of in the meantime. Since there was only a small coffee shop in the area, Spook would sit and watch Jones from there.

Dennis was about to pay Peterson when Jones came back out with a duffle over his shoulder. He hailed a cab so they were back to following him. The cab took Jones to a car rental lot; this wasn't what Spook had expected, so he was immediately on the phone to the Lattimers for help getting a tracking device, since he had used his last one on Giovanni.

As Jones came out and went to a late model SUV, Spook asked Peterson to continue to follow him once again, until one of the Lattimers could get what they needed and meet up with Spook. Jones pulled out of the lot and headed west! What the hell!

Chapter 32

About twenty-five minutes later, Jones pulled over at a gas station to fill the big rig with fuel and some food and drinks for himself. Nick and Spook took that opportunity to place the tracker on his rig. They had taken time a few miles back for Spook to finally pay Peterson, and get in the truck with Nick. They got lucky with the traffic being slow enough, so they didn't have to worry about losing Jones. Nick's rig was fully loaded with their own bags, drinks and food to carry them for a long stretch.

Dennis didn't want to take the chance to get physically any closer to Jones, in case he had seen him back in Chicago. Nick went in the convenience store while Spook made quick work of the back door of Jones' SUV, to look around. His duffle was mostly clothes, but there was a small case which Spook knew was for a pistol. Placing a tag on the gun case and one inside the SUV was about as good as it was going to get. There should be one on a clothing item too, but it was too hard to decide what he might use. A quick glance to the store, showed that Jones was coming out; with any luck Nick, would be able to stall him long enough for Spook to get out of the truck.

Long after the sun went down, Jones finally pulled into a motel. He had been heading steadily toward JJ. Subsequently, after many phone calls to everyone, JJ had been told about Jones coming that direction and what to do as precautions. Thumper got a plane out and was also headed toward his own home; he wasn't going to take any chance that Michaella was unprotected either.

Gage and Nate stayed on the alert with Giovanni. They hadn't been able to move in and arrest him, since they didn't have back up as the local agents had seemed to have other cases all of a sudden. It was too telling that the agents here were on Giovanni's payroll.

Nate didn't want to mess anything up with the arrest and have the psychopath back on the street, without being tried and convicted. All they could hope for at this point, was that Giovanni would screw up and find himself in cuffs on his way to a cell or dead. Dennis hoped the latter, since scum should be disposed of, not given a warm bed and three squares a day.

Nate hadn't seen Giovanni and started to wonder if he was still in his room. A physical check from Gage told them Giovanni wasn't in his room and had disappeared again; they figured he'd gotten out of the hotel somehow unseen. Geek had been put on the mission to find him as quick as possible, which unfortunately was on a plane headed west, also toward JJ. Geek had been able to find out that he would be landing in only minutes, not far from the town where she was. Somehow, they had found where JJ was and it wouldn't be long before they closed in on her. The only thing to do now was beat them there.

Spook and Nick weren't going to take any chances on losing Jones so didn't bother sleeping. They discussed splitting up or both staying on Jones. Since getting a second vehicle here would be impossible, they would stay together. After barely two hours, Jones got back in his rig and pulled back out on the highway, still heading west. At this rate, he would be at the Wisconsin boarder and within reach of JJ by sun up. Was he planning on meeting up with Giovanni or going straight to JJ?

Dennis did the only thing he could think of without drawing attention to themselves: he called the local sheriff's department to report a suspicious driver. He didn't know if it would work, but it would slow the man down until they could get more people there. Not knowing this particular counties' law officers didn't help, but he knew the ones where he lived and that was his next call. Approximately ten minutes later, they were passed by a deputy with his lights on, pulling

Jones over. They drove on by, making sure they didn't look toward the officer or Jones. They continued pushing on toward JJ.

Only minutes after they went by Jones, Thumper called to tell them he had picked up the truck from Michaella's house in town and was headed toward his house. He had called and the ladies were still up at Dennis's cabin. Even though Reed had walked up from Thumper's, they didn't have to worry about footprints leaving a trail since the falling and blowing snow had already filled in his tracks.

Dennis directed Nick to pull over and they switched seats. Driving through back roads, some that were still buried from the constantly falling snow, Dennis was able to move them along faster than navigating from the shotgun seat. Snow was the best deterrent for city slickers like Giovanni and hopefully Jones, but Dennis and Thumper had lived in weather like this too long to not have it hinder their movements.

Dennis wasn't really surprised at the amount of snow that had fallen since they had left weeks ago; living in this part of the country most of his life, he knew how mother nature was always unpredictable. Within minutes, Dennis was on the road driving toward his town. He pointed out the tracks indicating Thumper's progress from Michaella's. The plows were already moving the snow off of the main roads, and the town was coming alive as only these people knew how to do, day in and day out, during the winter.

Pulling over at the local hardware store, Dennis moved to get out. "I'll be right back!"

Jumping down into a foot of fresh, light snow fall, he moved quickly, saying hello to the kid shoveling off the side walk in front of the store. Coming out only minutes later, he was laden down with heavier winter gear and snow shoes. With all of his own gear at his cabin, he had to have enough to get him up there. Nick just shuddered at the thought of using snow shoes, but didn't say a word.

It was a slow process driving through the snow and congestion of the other locals trying to get where they too were going. Holding his curses back, Dennis did what he could to make it to the road below Thumper's cabin. He parked at the same spot where Michaella had gone over the edge only months before. Pulling on the heavier coat, hat and gloves, he cast a look at Nick.

"Are you coming or staying here?" Dennis asked Nick again. They had already discussed a plan on the drive from the hardware store. Spook would hike up the hill from below, leaving Nick to make sure no one got past him on this road, which was one of the two going up to the homes above the river. The other road would be less traveled and hard to navigate, unless you knew it well enough.

"Are you kidding?" Nick said. "I'll stay here and slow anyone down that I can. Just be careful!" Nick was already pulling out his phone to call his brother for an update.

Dennis was laughing as he stood on the road putting on his set of snow shoes. With the door still open he smiled at Nick, "Careful? Really? I have tromped around in a lot worse. Getting from here to Thumper's is the easy part. From his cabin to mine will be the hard part, since I will have more trees to contend with." Resettling his cap, he continued, "Thumper has already been by here, so he'll be on the hill with me. We won't hesitate to draw a gun on Giovanni if he shows up. The sheriff's name is Carson if he shows up. Explain more of what is going on and he will do what he can to help. For now, stay with the truck and keep your eyes open. Jones is one tricky bastard and I wouldn't put it past him to be breathing down our back after being pulled over."

With one quick look up the hill, Dennis asked, "Any questions?"

Nick, too looked up the hill, took out his pistol and was about to hand it to Spook when the door was closed. Dennis showed his own gun before heading up the hill. Nick was on his own.

Chapter 33

Spook was met at the back door of the cabin by Thumper. Clothed in winter hunting gear, Thumper held out a cup of coffee to his best friend.

"Figured you could use this!"

Spook took the first sip tentatively, to see just how hot it was. It hadn't cooled too much, telling him just how long Thumper had been there. He drank the rest quickly before it cooled completely. He would need it.

"I saw the truck below and estimated how long it would take you to get here." Thumper said as they walked toward the shed. "What more do we know about Jones and Giovanni?"

Spook waited while his friend unlocked the shed door and they stepped inside. With a flick of a few switches, lights flashed on as well as a heater purring to warm the space. Thumper walked over to a large locked cabinet. He spun the combination lock, swiftly rotated it with the right numbers and opened it to reveal quite a load of munitions and other gear they would need, including more winter camo.

"Giovanni slipped by Gage and Nate. Geek spotted him getting on a plane headed this way. He should be on the ground, but we have no idea as to who he is meeting or what he is doing. Jones was pulled over by the St. Croix sheriff a while ago; an unanimous tip of a felon carrying a weapon. We would have to call Carson to see if anything came of it. For now, let's get up to my place."

"I called Reed twenty minutes or so ago and told him to expect us," Thumper said before he tossed Spook a bullet proof vest, pair of white coveralls and jacket as he pulled out a spotting scope and rifle. He checked the battery on the scope and laid out several clips for the rifle. Next, he grabbed a shot gun and a box of shells.

"How are they holding up?" Spook knew he didn't have to say

the women's names, Thumper had already gathered the meaning of the question.

"They're good, at least as far as Reed could tell. If we stopped gabbing like old women, we could be on the way." Thumper took the dirty look he got as a sign that his buddy wasn't in the mood for razzing of any kind. He just chuckled to Spook's back.

After Spook had on the white clothes, he shouldered the rifle and pocketed the full clips. They were so used to working with each other, no talking was necessary to know who would be carrying what and how they would approach the situation. Lastly, Thumper opened a small handheld case with their radio equipment and ear buds, putting one in his ear and handing one to Spook, who did the same. Grabbing a backpack, Thumper put the shells, extra pistol rounds and the radio in it before shouldering it and strapping it around his chest. He put the spotting scope in the inside pocket of his coat to keep it dry and protected.

As soon as they were both readied, they stepped out in the yard. Thumper locked the shed, went to the house and secured it also. There was no way they would give anyone the advantage of what was in any of his buildings.

Moving slowly, methodically, they worked their way up the hill towards Spook's cabin. Thumper taking the right and Spook flanking on the left. The tracks Reed had made were between them and nearly covered from the wind, which had blown the snowfall around. They were only half way to the cabin when the wind picked up again and was blowing more of the new snow around, filling in their tracks as well, making white out conditions.

Before cresting the last few feet, Spook stopped and gave a hand signal to Thumper, who took out the spotting scope and canvased the area. It was quiet, almost too quiet. There was very little smoke coming from the chimney, telling them there wasn't much of a fire in the fireplace. Something wasn't right. Cautiously, they preceded the rest of the way on their bellies, crawling so as to not alert anyone of their presence.

There was a single set of tracks in the yard behind a Hummer. The vehicle was big and heavy, making it able to drive through the amount of snow that had already fallen. It had to have come up the other road, since there was only one set of tracks below Thumper's place. As they crawled slowly up behind it, they saw three sets of footprints leading toward the cabin. One set to the front and the others to the back. At the front there was a window broken and front door was standing only slightly ajar.

Inwardly, Spook smiled at that. If the alarm was set and the window broken, an alarm would have sounded at the sheriff's office. As a longtime friend of Thumper's, the sheriff would have to check it out knowing how close they were. There was no way he would ignore the alarm because Thumper would never let him hear the end of it.

Thumper pulled the scope out again and looked toward the door, hoping to see something either through the door or the window. What he did see, didn't bode well for someone. Carefully, he handed the scope to Spook and pointed toward the wood piled on the small porch. As clear as the nose on his face, Spook saw the blood and the imprint of a fallen person, along with drag marks to the door. Then all Spook saw was the red of anger.

Either it was the blood of Reed or that of one of the women. More than likely Reed. He would have heard the vehicle and went out to see who it was, only to be ambushed. But what happened then? If Reed had gone out, had he disengaged the alarm or counted on the minute delay to arouse the silent alarm in the sheriff's department.

Their best plan, would be to go after the two who had gone around back first. They slithered back to the edge of the hill and moved on to the take a different means to the back of the cabin. Thumper moved down the hill and around the front toward the back while Spook moved toward his own shed. Going behind it, he pulled his phone out and quickly sent a text to Gage apprising him of the situation. Help would come, but would it be on time?

Moving stealthily, Spook was able to gain ground quickly and was in sight of the back door. It wasn't open, but again a window had been broken. Taking every precaution, he moved next to the large wood pile.

Warily, he whispered Thumper's name, when he got a "Go" he said, "Can you see anything from where you are?"

"Negative! No one is outside. You?"

"A window is broke, the door closed." Looking around, there was only one way in unnoticed, but he would have to leave most of his gear here behind the wood pile. "Thumper, I have a tunnel to the cabin. I will have to leave most of my gear here though, to make it through. I will let you know when I am to the door into the cabin. Be my eyes out here!"

"Affirmative, be safe, friend."

Swiftly, Spook shed what wasn't needed and covered it the best he could. Next to the wood pile was the well pump cover and the opening to the tunnel. Hurriedly, he lifted the lid and slid in, knowing that this access to the cabin couldn't be seen from any of the windows. Just to be sure, he wasn't wasting any time, moving rapidly, first through the door and then the tunnel itself. The tunnel was only thirty yards long and he had been cunning enough to lay down wood planks the whole length of it. He had planned to make it bigger and line the walls and ceiling too, just hadn't really made the time to complete it. Having the SEAL training still ingrained in him, Spook had also added a steel box inside the tunnel, just in case, which held a few more surprises that just may come in handy.

At the hatch to the cabin entrance, Spook pulled his phone and opened the app for his cameras for a look around. Mentally punching himself for not doing it earlier, he flipped through each room. His bedroom, where he would enter the cabin, the guest room and the bathroom were clear. There was someone looking out the backdoor in the kitchen and another at the front door. The last man, Giovanni, was sitting in Spook's Lazy-Boy in the living room. The women were huddled on the sofa and Reed was bound and laying at their feet. It looked as if he was unconscious, a good-sized gash on his head.

Relaying the information to Thumper, they decided on the best action. Taking out either of the men at the doors meant putting a bullet through a wall. The one in the kitchen was a better bet, which would give Spook time to get into position to take out the one at the front door. Spook gave him the best location for the shot, knowing that the weakest spot would be just outside of the doorframe itself.

They wondered if Reed was out or if he was playing possum. Thumper chuckled, "Let me try one of our animal calls, you watch for a reaction from Reed. If he does move, we have help inside."

"Let me get inside first. The hatch is in my bedroom closet, so give me five minutes then give Reed the signal. Then we can decide how to move."

"Ten-four."

Sliding the hatch was noiseless, as Spook knew it would be. Pulling himself up into a standing position, he checked his watch and found he still had two minutes before the signal. He reached down and opened the steel box, retrieved the Taser, extra hand gun and ammo. Spook knew from the earlier look at the camera that his footlocker holding his other gear was still under the bed, but didn't know if Giovanni and his men had found it or not. He would go on the belief that they had.

Outside, he heard the coyote call. Watching Reed closely, Spook saw him puff his cheeks twice quickly, so he relayed Thumper with that info before moving out of the closet. Since the closet was on the backside of the bathroom, it's door couldn't be seen unless you were actually in the bedroom. He carefully pushed the sliding door open and stepped into his own room before moving to his door, which stood open. He whispered the go signal for Thumper to drop the man in the kitchen in three after a second coyote call. This would alert Reed, even though he was bound, to be ready.

Spook knew he would only have one chance at the man at the door. If he was lucky, he might get a chance at Giovanni. He hoped he was because the man had been on this earth too long as it was. To hell with arresting him and taking him to trial, he had come too close to JJ this time. It was time to see to it that JJ wouldn't ever have to worry about the man again.

Chapter 34

It all happened so fast, JJ thought. First, she heard the coyote calls and then the shot in the kitchen. Before she had even realized what was happening, the man by the front door dropped and Dennis was in the living room, leaving only Giovanni to be dealt with. She was closest to him, so kicked quickly to try and knock the gun out of his hand, which he had been holding on Reed or Michaella, alternatively. He hadn't expected it, didn't have a tight grip on it, so the gun went flying back over his head.

When she made a move to stand, Giovanni produced a second gun from his coat pocket and aimed it toward her. She could see the hesitation in his eyes; whether to fire in the direction of the doorway, where the shot came, killing the man at the front door, or at his daughter. He fired two or maybe it was three rounds towards Dennis without even looking, keeping his eyes on her and moving out of the chair and going up against the wall of the kitchen. Of course, his shots missed. Dennis's aim didn't though! Dennis came in low as his training kicked in, and Giovanni had aimed high, as if someone would come in the room standing up.

A single round flew out of Dennis's gun, hitting Giovanni's shoulder! The round was a large caliber and nearly took the man's arm off. Dennis came fully into the room then, looking first at Giovanni as he bled on the floor, then to JJ with questions in his eyes. Dennis turned his attention back to Giovanni, not sure where the first gun had gone as he stumbled because of the hit he took. He didn't say anything as Michaella helped Reed up. Thumper came in the back, looking to Michaella. Her relief that he was there had her rushing to him, throwing herself in to his open arms. JJ looked at the two holding each other before looking back at Dennis. She wasn't sure

196

of herself or of him and what he might want from her. The spell was broken as soon as Giovanni tried to move toward her.

Dennis was swift in doling out punishment to the man who had caused JJ so much torment over the last few months, dropping him with one, well placed punch to the jaw. Giovanni fell like a load of bricks to the floor.

Stepping over him to the man lying dead by his front door, Dennis did a quick search, revealing that the man hadn't carried any ID, whatsoever. It wasn't Jones! Taking out his phone, he took a picture and sent it to Geek for an identity. Peering into the kitchen, Dennis saw the man there also laying on the floor. A look to Thumper, who shook his head in a negative manner, telling Dennis that he would have do the same with him to be identified.

It had been silent after those few gun shots, but now Dennis took control, starting with the questions. "Is everyone alright?" Looking toward Reed, he stated, "Doc, you aren't supposed to be the one bleeding!"

Dennis walked over to his friend to assess his injury before going to his footlocker and retrieving the first aid kit. He set it next to Reed who was now sitting on the coffee table. Thumper released Michaella and went to the fireplace to stoke the fire and adding wood. A roaring fire was soon taking over and the space inside the cabin was warming; dispelling more than the chill which came into the cabin along with Giovanni.

Michaella helped Reed get out some antiseptic wipes and gauze to clean and bandage his head, but the wound couldn't be cleaned correctly with wipes. Michaella finally talked Reed into going into the bathroom, so she could do a better job of checking his head. He was being a typical man and refusing, telling her he was fine. Being assertive and used to telling others to do something, Michaella had him up and moving.

JJ couldn't move, she just watched as the other four moved

around the cabin and took care of what needed to be done. Reed and Michaella had left the room, Thumper was working with the fire, Dennis moved the dead man out of the room, to the front stoop and closed the door before going into the kitchen to do the same there. He knew he would be put on the spot for moving the bodies, but he didn't want them in the room to continue upsetting the women.

It was all surreal to her; she had never personally seen a gun fight or seen a man die until recently, and now she'd seen too many. The speed at which it all had occurred, put her into a state of disbelief and numbness. Still standing in front of the couch, disconnected from her thoughts, JJ hadn't seen Giovanni stir. Before she knew what had happened, he had stood and wrapped his uninjured arm around her throat, so tight she could barely breathe.

Dennis came back at that moment, intent on binding Giovanni, to eliminate him as a threat, until the authorities arrived. When he saw JJ's pale, shocked face, he stopped dead in his tracks.

"Let go of her Giovanni! You have nowhere to go! With the way you are bleeding, I doubt you will even make it out to the truck."

Thumper had stood as soon as he heard Spook, turning in time to see the gun on the floor, but not in time to get to it before Giovanni had.

A sick kind of sound came out of his mouth before Giovanni stooped with JJ, to pick up the hand gun protruding out from under the couch. As he stood, he waved the gun at Dennis, motioning him to move away from the door.

"Get back or I will put a bullet in her." Giovanni spit out.

When Dennis still hadn't moved, Giovanni flicked the safety off with his thumb. "I said get back."

Carefully and very slowly, Dennis moved farther into the living room. He knew there was no way the man was going anywhere; he had the keys for the hummer in his own pocket, garnered from the dead man in the kitchen. He would just have to wait the man out.

Either he would bleed to death, on his floor, or the sheriff would show up.

"Listen Giovanni, just drop the gun and we will help stop the bleeding from your shoulder."

Giovanni again scoffed at him, tightening his hold both on JJ and the gun.

Dennis tried another approach, "You aren't going to get out of here, what with the weather and the sheriff on the way."

Actually looking out the window, Giovanni said, "I'll get out of here. We cut the lines to the house. The is no way the sheriff will be coming; my beautiful daughter didn't have time to call and there is no cell service."

Laughter erupted from Dennis. JJ gave him an odd look, wondering why that was so funny.

"You may have cut lines, but not the ones that counted. See, the alarm isn't wired with the rest of the house. It's on a circuit all on its own, directly to the sheriff's office, should a door or window become broken. And since the sheriff is a personal friend to Thumper here, he is probably already using the tracks you made, to drive right up to the cabin."

"You lying scum! There is no way a little alarm will bring the sheriff out under these conditions."

Thumper grinned now. "Want to put money on that dirtbag?"

Dennis saw the shadow in the bathroom door, but knew Reed would stay there until he was really needed. His mind was racing, trying to come up with a fast plan to get JJ away from the man who had become such a threat to her life.

Quietly, he tried again looking at the wound as blood continued to flow from it. There wasn't much of a chance the man would be standing much longer with the amount of blood he was losing. "Giovanni, Reed is a medic. He could bandage your wound. If not, you will more than likely bleed to death, even before the sheriff arrives."

"Get back, I said." Giovanni actually spit the words out. He swayed slightly before leaning their weight up against the wall for balance.

This couldn't be happening was all JJ could think. She was helpless and couldn't do anything to get in the way. She would have to trust Dennis, he wouldn't let anything happen to her.

Taking a different tactic once again, Dennis asked, "How in the hell were you even able to find JJ? We know about Jones, but I think he is in trouble of his own making at the moment."

There was a sick chuckle from Giovanni. "I have always known where my Maria was. Her mother couldn't hide her from me."

The man was getting more unsteady on his feet. With the puddle forming on the floor, it wouldn't be long before he either passed out due to blood loss or died completely.

"How could that be? The records for her adoption were sealed. JJ didn't go by her birth name and she had never found her mother." Dennis paused. "How could you know where she was?" He asked the question again.

Giovanni had the coldest gleam in his eyes now and Dennis was glad JJ couldn't see it. His ugly, disdainful laugh bounced off the walls of the small cabin. "She was just like a prized dog or horse." Giovanni spat on the floor, making an ugly blood-drool mark next to his own foot. "Within hours of her birth, she had an electronic chip implanted in her hip. I have always known where she was! I knew every movement she made. I kept close tabs on her as she reached maturity, so she could be of use to me." Taking a slow breath, Giovanni demanded, "Now, get back!"

JJ paled even more. She knew exactly where this chip was since she had always wondered how she came to have the little, almost unnoticeable scar on her left hip. Then her world was moving, literally, in a different direction as Giovanni started to slide to the floor. Before he got there, Dennis was pulling the gun out of his hand and pulling JJ into his strong arms, and around the corner to the kitchen.

Thumper moved over to Giovanni to check for a pulse as Reed came out of the bathroom with Michaella on his heels. The wounded man had lost too much blood, his pulse was faint and his breathing was shallow. Reed grabbed the first aid kit, hoping to help the dying man. Michaella went back to the bathroom for more towels, but as she handed them to Reed, he shook his head knowing it was already too late. Taking a large towel, he covered Giovanni's face and upper torso.

They all exhaled as they heard the sheriff's siren come into the yard. Help had arrived, late as it was.

Chapter 35

Dennis insisted on Thumper taking the women down to his house while the sheriff's department, detectives and coroner took care of the bodies and evidence. An ambulance took Reed to the hospital, despite his protests that he was fine. JJ was glad to be out of the way; she wanted to bring her thoughts and emotions back under control.

To think that her father had her tagged like a dog when she had been born was appalling. Now, she really believed he was the monster her mother had feared. Having him know every move she had made, all of her life, was a testament to his vile intent for her all along. Like her mother, she was nothing but a pawn to him, to be there for him as he needed. It was a wonder he had waited so long to find a use for her. She was glad he was dead; having wanted to see him stand trial and go to jail for her mother' murder, would always be at the back of her mind. She was sure the federal DA would be just as disappointed in the loss, because of the many charges they had wanted to file against him. As she thought of it though, he would have found a way to make prison work for him too, not finding the discomfort as most would in the same situation.

As they talked it over on the way down the hill, at least at this point, Giovanni's organization had been decimated with him gone. Paul said by the Lattimers account, most of his men scattered and were in the wind, when they found out he had ordered Marco to be killed. That he had not used his own men was a demonstration of the lack of confidence he found in his own people. Nate had hoped that they would be able to find some of Giovanni's men, and hold some of them accountable for their acts, but he was just being optimistic at most.

There was also enough evidence to have the all of the corrupt officials taken into custody. The city of New York wouldn't be the only place in the process of filling the vacancies of all of those officials. Perhaps now, more people would come forward and offer testimony against the dead Giovanni, his henchmen and the other people responsible for him having the power that he had held.

Walking into Paul's house again left JJ completely exhausted. Michaella could see it, more than anyone else, what a toll this had taken on her friend. With the suggestion of a hot bath and a soothing tea, Michaella showed her to the guest room, putting her bag on the bed. Telling her to take her time, Michaella said she would see to some tea and perhaps a light fare of crackers and cheese, until Dennis returned.

JJ was pretty sure she wouldn't be able to stomach any food for a while, still remembering how her father looked as he died. She walked into the adjoining bathroom and ran a tub full of hot water. Removing her clothes, she noted the amount of blood on them. She couldn't fathom ever wearing them again, so balled them up and dropped them in the garbage can. She slid into the hot water and let it take away some of her tension. Staying there until the water was cold, JJ got out and wrapped a large towel around herself. She had no energy left, so climbed into the inviting and waiting bed. She was asleep as soon as her head hit the pillow.

Dennis was done talking to Nick, the sheriff, detectives and coroner! All he wanted was a shower, a hot meal and a bed, preferably in that order. He had finally got the permission to leave, so had to ask one of the deputies for a ride down the hill to Paul's place. Sauntering up the back stairs, he was met in the kitchen by Paul himself and watched as Michaella rose from the couch in front of the fireplace, walked over to door of the kitchen, waited.

Paul handed him three fingers of brandy, letting him drink it before the few questions he had would begin. Dennis downed it in one swallow, a validation of the repulsive time he had, dealing with the dead in his house and the local authorities.

"So, is it over? Are the powers to be going to put this to bed, or are we going to have to get the federal DA up here to sort it out?"

Taking the brandy bottle himself, he poured another three fingers and downed it once again. Not really accustomed to drinking hard liquor, Dennis had to take a breath before answering.

"It's done. I placed the call to Hankinson myself just to clear the matter up. Jones is in custody for a felon possessing a firearm. He is sitting in a cell as we speak. I think the local DA will not go lightly on him. The conspiracy to commit murder and possession charges won't go away even though Giovanni is dead. They have Jones' cell phone with Giovanni's phone calls recorded on it. The man was even dumb enough to save a voice mail from Giovanni with the arrangement for the bank transfer, along with account numbers to wire money to." Dennis shook his head and looked around. "How is JJ taking all of this?"

Michaella stepped up to Paul's side and took the glass from him, taking the last bit of brandy before setting it down. "She's went to taking a bath to relax. She's shaken and exhausted." Michaella looked at both men, one in turn. "JJ actually paled when I mentioned food. I wouldn't be surprised if she crawled right into the bed."

Dennis understood, he couldn't blame her one bit. "Thumper, can I use your shower to get the stink off?"

Paul nodded and handed over a small duffle he had grabbed from the car. Dennis moved through the house just has he had done a thousand times. He paused at the closed door to one of the guest rooms. More than anything, he wanted to join JJ, but needed time of his own to settle down before he did that. Stepping to the other guest room, Dennis tossed his bag on the bed, opened it and grabbed clean jeans and underwear. Heading into the bathroom, he turned on the shower to let it warm a little as he undressed.

Dropping everything in a heap on the floor, he released a sigh as he stepped under the hot spray of the shower. He let his mind quickly run through the facts, sorted them out and stored them for later thought. Emptying his mind, he wanted only good thoughts and feelings when he saw JJ again. There was so much they needed to talk about and none of it had to do with the scum of a father she had. Once he was sure he had himself under control, anger gone and positive thoughts in place, Dennis turned off the shower.

After drying and putting on his clean clothes, he shaved and made sure he was once again presentable. He checked himself in the mirror, making sure he was mentally ready to see the woman who had come to mean so much to him. He left the bedroom and walked back to the kitchen.

Paul had made a quick fare for their meal; hot ham and cheese sandwiches and his mom's home canned chicken soup. He had become quite the cook over the last few years and Dennis was glad for it. He had been eating better, and enjoyed ribbing his best friend about being so domestic, considering how big Thumper was. His best friend took it with a smile, knowing Dennis couldn't top the meals he was consuming.

Dennis noticed JJ wasn't in the kitchen or the living room. He was about to go get her, when Michaella stopped him, touching him lightly on his arm.

"Dennis, let her be!" She said quietly. "If she's hungry, she will come out." She smiled at him, "Sit down and eat. We'll let her rest, I'm sure she needs some time after what happened today."

Dennis didn't like it, but would do as Michaella asked. JJ did need some time! She didn't have the training that he or Paul had. JJ wouldn't know how to let it go as he did in the shower. Dennis would give her some time, but then they would have to work through her thoughts and feelings, so she could heal and move on. Yes, he'd give her some time.

They sat down and ate the nourishing food, talked about what had happened at his house, and laughed over the way Reed didn't want to go to the hospital. It was about time they had something on their corpsman, since he had enough on all of them and their teammates. As if on que, Paul's phone rang.

Looking at it he smiled, "Hey, Doc! How are you doing?" He listened, nodded and smiled. "Sure, one of us will come and get you. You can stay here for a few days." Again, he listened. "Great, we'll be there in about thirty minutes. Hold tight!"

Paul disconnected the phone and set it aside before getting up. Efficiently, he cleared the table. "One of us needs to run and get him before the nurses get any ideas." He chuckled, shook his head, "Reed said one of them already offered him their own couch. That man needs a good woman to take care of him. Lord knows he's taken care of all of us too long. He's due for a little pampering!"

Paul gave a secret look to Michaella, and they were both thinking Lauren, Michaella's best friend, could be that woman.

Dennis stood and went to get his coat, "Thumper, give me keys! I'll go and get him. I could use the time to think."

Michaella and Paul exchanged another look, but didn't disagree with their friend. Paul took the keys out of his pocket and dropped them in the waiting hand Dennis held out.

Shaking hands with Paul, Dennis then took Michaella in a hug, whispering in her ear, "Take care of JJ for me while I'm gone." He had no doubt that she would, but voiced it anyway. He slipped out the door and out to the garage to Thumper's truck.

Chapter 36

JJ stirred in the bed, which was almost too comfortable. Although she could have stayed in bed longer, her stomach growled telling her it hadn't been fed for a while. Rolling over, she realized she hadn't even put on her sleep shirt. Remembering her fatigue after her shower, she had just crawled into bed and went right to sleep. Glancing at the clock, she was aghast at how long she had slept, as it was the wee hours of the night, or morning as it were.

Quietly, she dressed in jogging pants and sweatshirt with her feet sheathed in just socks. Going to the closed door, cautiously, she opened it and peered out the hall. The rest of the house was quiet, with only a light on over the sink in the kitchen. Being careful not to make any noise, JJ walked toward the kitchen, and just about screamed when she saw someone sitting in a chair, in the dark. A small movement in that direction brought another light on above the table. JJ blinked at the brightness and the sight of Dennis, as he stood and came toward her.

Approaching her, Dennis enfolded her in his embrace. It felt so natural to him to have her there. It was at that precise moment, he knew she had been made for him and him for her. This was how it felt to have a soul mate. He took a deep breath, released it and her, holding her at arm's length.

"Hungry?" Dennis asked quietly.

JJ nodded, but still held on to him. Knowing then she had just felt something she had never felt before; she was reluctant to let go. It was more than a sense of rightness, it was a belonging.

Stepping into the kitchen, Dennis pulled out the leftover chicken soup and makings for sandwiches for them. After setting the soup on the stove to warm, he built them both a sandwich, poured milk and got bowls and spoons. Setting their places at the bar, he made it feel like when they did this at Christmas so many years ago, and before she had been kidnapped. He hoped they could rekindle some of those same feelings. When the soup was hot, they both sat down to the silence of the kitchen, comfortable with each other.

They fell into a very casual conversation, avoiding what had happened the day before. There would be time enough for that later Dennis thought. Right now, he needed to make sure they were good; to their relationship could move forward. He was sure she would know when they could talk about her father, hoping it would not come too soon as he wanted this quiet, intimate time alone with her.

As the sun started to come up, Dennis released a huge yawn, blinked and looked at the clock. JJ also looked at the clock as she slid off the stool and took his hand.

"Let's get some sleep," she stated as she moved them toward the room she had come from.

Once in the room, they slid under the covers. Dennis tucked her next to him and closed his eyes. It didn't take him long to fall into a deep sleep, knowing she was there and safe.

JJ on the other hand, let her mind wander for a long time before sleep also took her. She had thought he would want to discuss what had happened in his house, but he had left the topic off the table. She supposed they would talk more today, and the authorities would want more information from her. They would all deal with it later. For now, it was important to figure out where she was going to go from here, and would Dennis be with her. She smiled, reached up and touched his face. Remembering how sleeping with him before all this started, brought her the comfort she needed again so she too went to sleep.

They were wakened by a knock on the door. Dennis replied in a sleepy voice to go away. The knock came again. This time JJ told the person on the other side to come in. Thumper stuck his head in.

"Spook, Hankinson and Gage are on the phone. Move your butt buddy and come out here." He smiled at JJ as she rolled over and looked at him, "Morning JJ! Did you sleep well?"

"Morning Paul! Yes, I did, thank you!" JJ slid out of bed and went into the bathroom. As she closed the door, she heard some very directed cuss words from Dennis; directed to his best friend. She couldn't hear Paul's response because he had already walked away from the door.

Dennis flipped the blankets off, sat up and put his feet on the floor. He looked over at the clock on the table next to the bed, and he was surprised at how late it was. They had slept all of the morning and part of the afternoon away. It was already three in the afternoon, with the sun even now starting to sink beyond the trees.

JJ came out of the bathroom, hair combed and as beautiful as a model, even in her sweats. He stood and wrapped an arm around her, gave her a quick kiss. She had brushed her teeth and tasted minty. Dennis smiled down at her and released her and stepped into the bathroom himself. When he came out, the bed was made and the room empty. He couldn't help but laugh as he walked toward the others in the kitchen.

There was a phone on the counter, Dennis assumed it was on speaker since everyone was gathered around it.

Paul looked at his friend, smirked and said, "Rip Van Winkle just came in, if you want to repeat that Hankinson."

The comment earned Paul a swift slug to the shoulder, but there was no heat behind it. The men had been friends too long to have a simple comment upset either of them. JJ just smiled in return as she took a cup of coffee from Michaella, who also handed one to Dennis.

JJ listened to the conversations going back and forth in the room and the phone. She was amazed at the speed to which the investigation had flowed once she had gotten them the information from the safety deposit box her mother had set up. Multiple arrests had already been made in New York with more to follow. They had actually found some of Giovanni's men and they were singing like canaries to keep their own sentences in prison short. They had also arrested the man responsible for kidnapping her and carting her off to New York. They were still working on the officials and agents in Chicago that had ties to Giovanni, but Hankinson thought they would have more arrests coming there in a few days.

JJ slipped out of the room, grabbing her jacket from the peg to step outside. She needed some fresh air, because the talk about her father was sickening her once more. All she wanted was this drama to be over. The man was dead, but the ordeal would be a long time in dying.

She started walking around the wrap-around deck, noticed that the snow had stopped, taking in the pleasure of hearing the birds happily chirp in the trees. A quick motion caught her eye. As she turned her head, a pair of squirrels scurried around a tree, playing with each other. JJ smiled as she watched them, back and forth, up and down, round and round. She didn't hear the door open and close on the other end of the deck.

Dennis stepped out and saw his woman smiling at squirrels playing in the yard. With all that she had been through lately, she could still find enjoyment in something so simple. Carefully, as not to startle her, he moved up behind her and enveloped her within his embrace. With her back to his chest, his head rested on the top of hers. Dennis felt her sigh and had to do so himself.

"You look so peaceful out here, I hated to ruin it." Dennis said.

"It wasn't ruined!" JJ turned to look at him over her shoulder. "I just couldn't take any more talk about him." She looked back to where the squirrels had been. "Is it over? Can I be rid of the fear now or will I have to worry about his competitors coming after me?"

Dennis turned her toward him. "JJ, as far as the authorities can gauge, it's over. We will do everything to protect you. When

Reed heard about the tracking chip, he said he could help you have it removed, safely and destroyed. Since we already had the new identity built for you, if you would like, we can still move forward to putting you into that identity." He watched for her reaction before continuing. "By your original plan, you have left your old life and can start a new one. Michaella's offer still stands and I think you should consider it."

JJ was still, contemplating his words. It was easy for him to say, harder for her to put into her own mind, after all that had happened. It had been easier to start over when she had set the plan into action. But now, she just wasn't as sure. She supposed it would be the best to start completely over and she didn't have any doubt she and Michaella would make a great team.

"Do you really think I should become someone else?" she asked.

"JJ," Dennis started, he knew was treading on new territory here. "JJ, you would only be changing your name, so your father's affiliates wouldn't be able to find you. More than likely, that wouldn't happen, but why take the chance. As far as we have been able to find out, there wasn't any open evidence of you within his home or office." He leaned into and kissed her lightly. "Let's take a drive and talk about this, some place that is private and much warmer."

She was starting to get cold and could use some time away from the others, so nodded yes. The time had come to talk and move on. It was time to put it all behind her.

Smiling, Dennis stepped inside grabbing keys to a truck and yelled they were taking a drive. Since he wanted complete privacy, and could think of only one place that wasn't his house, after starting the truck, went back to the house. Only moments later, he was back out and behind the wheel. Turning the truck around, he headed down the hill and toward town. She hadn't asked where they were going, trusting him and his knowledge of the town. JJ was surprised when they pulled up to Michaella's house.

Parking in the driveway, up next to the garage, Dennis got out and came around to the passenger door and helped JJ down. They walked together to the back door, where he took out a key and unlocked it. Once inside, she watched as he disengaged the security system, but wondered why he didn't reset it. Realizing the threat to her was now gone, she smiled inwardly to herself.

Dennis helped her off with her coat, hanging both on the coat tree in the entryway. Taking her hand, he led her into the kitchen, over to the table. After she sat down, he went back to the fridge to see if there was anything to drink in it. He was surprised to see a bottle of wine, so grabbed two glasses out of the cupboard and went to the table. Dennis shot her a smile as he grabbed a sealed container on the counter; it was full of cookies.

After pouring the glasses, he handed one to her. When JJ took hers, he offered her a toast. "To days less dramatic than the ones we've just lived through!" He touched his glass to hers, with a twinkle in his eyes.

"Amen to that!" JJ whispered.

Smiling, Dennis let the silence stretch out several more seconds, hoping she would open up and talk to him. He wasn't disappointed when she did just that.

"Dennis, I was resigned to starting a new life to get away from Giovanni, even before I knew it was him. I think without the help I got from Michaella, I wouldn't have been able to do that, so I guess I really owe her for her help."

"Michaella won't like hearing that you feel you owe her," he said.

"I know, but that is the way I feel right now. Just as I feel the same toward you and Paul. There is no way I can repay all that has been done to get me out of his clutches. And I will have to live with the death of Marco. If he had just told me, just once during those times I asked about what my father was really after." She shook her head. "I'm sure he knew, he just wouldn't tell me. Maybe if he had, he would still be alive today."

"JJ," Dennis started softly, "Don't do this to yourself. Marco was a full-grown man. He made his choices, which only partially led to his own death. None of that is on you!"

JJ dropped her eyes to the table, somewhere knowing he was right. Still, she would never forget a man was dead because of her.

Reaching over, Dennis lightly lifted her chin so she would look at him. "You don't have to make any decisions today or tomorrow, for that matter. Okay?"

He waited for her to answer, all he got was a nod of her head. Dennis could tell this was as hard on her today as it had been the day Marco died. He needed to change the topic and take it away from the Marco and what happened to him.

Lacing his fingers with hers, he wanted to really figure out where her heart was with their relationship. "JJ, let's forget about your dad for now and talk about us. I want to spend more time with you. When we first came to help you, I started remembering our nights all those years ago. Back then, you were the only person who got me, understood me and connected with me. I would like to see if that chemistry is still there."

With Dennis saying it like he had, brought back those memories and had her smiling once more. She relished those nights, where they sat quietly talking and building a friendship. Even then, she felt more with him than she had with anyone else, even Michaella, and rekindling that was something she too wanted.

"Tell me what you want, JJ, what's in your mind for your future." Dennis took her hand and brought it to his lips. "Let me see if I can deliver it for you."

The gesture had brought tears to her eyes. No one has ever treated her with such kindness and love. And love it was, she felt now for him. She guessed she always had, right from the start. He had been a friend first, but now she was touched more deeply. More could be said, she didn't know if she had the words, but she had to try.

"Dennis, you have always been so kind to me. When my own family had ignored me, you were there. When I asked for nothing, you gave me a sweater. When I was scared, you stayed on my couch for my protection and comfort. I have never, with anyone, had the connection I have with you. I can't explain it, how deep you are in my heart."

It was all he needed! Reaching over, he brought her closer, kissing her softly at first then with more heat. There was nothing more that he wanted but to solidify what they had with intimacy. They would have time for such a little later.

"Come here," he said as he lifted her to his lap. "With the holidays coming, Paul and I always spend some time out west with Gage's family. Our friend Belinda and Carrick had a new baby a while back. Would you come with us, go back and spend time there? Paul and Michaella are getting married soon. Belinda will need help with planning the wedding, with the baby and Liam taking up her time. What do you think?"

Resting her head on his shoulder, she couldn't imagine walking away from him or Michaella, as far as that goes. The answer would be the start for them and their future. She wanted that and him, what they could make together.

"Dennis," she looked at him directly, "I think I would like that. I don't really want to be alone, here or anywhere. Dennis," she started, then looked away, trying to come up with the words.

Dennis took her face in his hands. "What honey?" he asked.

"Dennis, I want what Paul and Michaella have. I see them and wonder at the deep bond they have and they haven't been together to long. I see them and know theirs will be a lasting love, with children and grandchildren. Until recently, until I asked Michaella to help me, and when she came with Paul, and I watched them, I had never realized I wanted just that." JJ reached over and took one of the glasses of wine, brought it to her lips.

"Oh, JJ. You can have that! We can have that!" He cuddled her close to his chest. "I hadn't thought I would ever have that until you came back into my life. We just have to want the same things!"

"Dennis, how I could have the same, coming from the background that I did. I was loved by my birth mother, yet given up, tolerated by my adoptive family and about to be used by my birth father to further his business?"

"Your birth mother loved you enough to get you away from your father, knowing she would never see you again. And nothing against the Hanson's, but I think they tried, the best they could. What about the Willis'? They loved you enough to see that you had shelter and food, loving you like you were a part of their family. I think if you take a close look inside, you will see how much all of them have made you who and what you are."

Sitting snuggly in his arms, she felt more loved than she had ever had in her whole life. She knew he spoke the truth. It was her turn, to voice the truth in her own heart.

"Dennis, I love you. Right from the start as we were kids, I knew I loved you." JJ leaned back to see his face as she said the words from her heart.

Dennis smiled, took her face and kissed her sweetly. "I love you too, JJ.

Epilogue

JJ stood on the porch of Carrick and Belinda's house, up in the Montana mountains, looking down at the valley below. It was probably the most beautiful view she had ever seen. Gazing down from here was like being at the top of the world. It made it easier to forget what the last few months had been like. The sun was high enough to give off shadows. The snow, which covered the slopes of the valleys and some of the trees, glistened and sparkled in the early morning sunshine. As winter here had taken the countryside, it was so different from what she had experienced in the St. Croix area surrounding Dennis and Paul's homes. It was so peaceful here, in the quiet winter; she would like to come back and see it during the summer to see if the same peace would come over her then.

They had left the Midwest a few days after the incident with Giovanni. She couldn't believe the speed the authorities had handled the circumstances of her father and his hired muscle. She had been completely left out of the whole affair. For this, she was so grateful to everyone. The complete evidence package she had turned over to the federal district attorney made that possible, and it was all undisputed. Hankinson saw no reason to involve her any deeper in the legalities, court cases and press. This would make it easier to move forward anonymously from the whole thing.

With what happened at Dennis's house, Michaella insisted JJ and Dennis stay at her house. It was nice to have the privacy, for them to solidify their relationship and deal with what might be coming because of her father. JJ took the time to decompress and come to terms of the identity change, and pull her thoughts toward what she wanted to do with her future and Michaella's proposition.

Dennis had shared all of the background they had put together for her new identity, and she realized it was a lot like her real self and what she had wanted, a chance to hide in plain sight. They had worked hard to make sure she wouldn't have to lie to a prospective new employer or company to find work. There was enough truth in the new persona, the only real change would be getting used to the new name, Lacey Daniels. Dennis thought she should start using it as soon as possible to make sure she would answer to it. They talked it over and told Paul and Michaella to start using it on the trip out west. A quick text to Gage, Reed and the Lattimers, would ensure everyone would be on the same page, regarding the new name.

On the private plane west, JJ and Michaella had time to talk about building a partnership in the consulting company, a lot like what Michaella had been doing before. Michaella was sure that JJ could step right in, and become a great colleague, assisting to developing the same kind of rapport as she had in the hotel business, or take it in any direction she felt comfortable with. Deciding to talk more as time allowed during the next few weeks, they tabled their dialog for now. They each had ideas and would take the time to explore them, put them to paper with pros and cons lists.

Going back and forth between Callahan's and Gage's, JJ enjoyed the large, loud and boisterous Thanksgiving weekend, filled with amazing food and new friends. The amount of fare Marlene, Gage's wife, set out for the meals for her family, the Callahan's and the four of them, staggered JJ. Since Belinda had the new baby and little Liam, Paul and JJ helped out as much as possible. Paul had become an amazing cook, bringing his own take on how something should be made; Marlena listened ribbing him about his eclectic sense of seasonings and spices.

They had all been surprised with the arrival of the Lattimers, along with Reed and Michaella's friend Lauren. The men laughed and told war stories enough to make them all laugh, until their sides were in stitches. The women worked on the wedding plans, right in front of the men, who seemed to be perplexed about the whole ordeal. For the most part, the men kept silent, only offering input when it came to the party after the ceremony. The decision had been made to have it take place there in the mountains, in the early spring. By then, Belinda would be back from maternity leave and able to spend more time with all the final details.

JJ liked both Belinda and Lauren upon their first meetings. She knew she had finally found people who could be lifelong friends and a new sort of family. The four of them laughed, talked and shared more intimate details of their lives, getting to know each other and their tastes. They complemented each other, in ways most people wouldn't understand. Coming together was as natural as breathing.

As the former concierge for one of the largest and most prestigious hotels in Chicago, JJ had knowledge to spare, in terms of putting personal touches on Michaella's wedding plans. Michaella and Paul wanted something small and intimate, simple yet elegant. JJ and Belinda looked at each other, laughed and walked off to put their heads together on it. JJ had no doubt that it would be a very beautiful event. She had looked through a portfolio of events Belinda had a hand in, and they were all wonderful. Working with her, Lauren and Michaella would be fun.

JJ turned as she heard the door from the four-season porch open. She smiled warmly at Dennis as he came toward her with two cups of coffee. Taking the offered cup and giving a kiss back, they settled on the swing overlooking the view. They were able to sit and enjoy each other without words. He had been watching her from the window for close to thirty minutes, wondering what she had been thinking about.

Dennis had noted how her composure had greatly changed since coming out to Montana. When she disappeared, he knew she could be found either in the nursery or here on the porch. JJ had confessed that she hadn't really wanted kids, but now, being with Liam and Belinda's sweet little girl, she had changed her mind. He would sit and watch her cuddle the pink bundle with love flowing out of her. He knew it wouldn't be long before he could give her children of their own.

Secretly, Dennis had gone into town with Gage to the little jewelry store and bought her an engagement ring and wedding band set. Planning to ask her on New Year's Eve, with a short, very short engagement, he wanted her attached to him permanently. They could wait until Paul and Michaella were wed before doing the same. Though now, he thought, why not have a dual ceremony? It would only make sense since the invite list would be about the same; it would make the need for travel less for their friends. He would put the question to Thumper and make sure he wouldn't rain on their parade.

"What were you thinking while you we standing out here?" Dennis asked after several minutes.

"Hmm," JJ turned and looked at him. "I was thinking about the view first. Then my mind went to the last few months, and how much something so dramatic could have such positive outcomes."

Jokingly, he asked, "Was I one of those positive outcomes?"

Smiling, JJ answered, "Yes!"

Returning her smile, he snuggled her closer to him. "Happy?"

"And then some!" she replied, kissing his cheek. "You?"

"JJ, you fill a space in my heart and soul. I had all but given up hope on finding someone as wonderful as you."

"Oh, Dennis! That is how I feel too. Can this really be happening?"

"In every way possible! Don't get any ideas on leaving me. I will always find you and bring you back to our home."

Again, she giggled, "No worries! I'm not leaving. But the same goes for you. If you leave, I will have Thumper and Gage hunt you down and bring you back."

With that said, he broke out in a 'throw your head back', belly rolling laugh. "I don't doubt it." Dennis scooped her into his arms, and walked with her back into the house to join the rest of the mayhem happening within.

They wouldn't have any problems being happy together, she thought, because they had been through hell and back. There was no way she, or him for that matter, would let anyone or anything come between them.

In the end, Dennis ended up bringing out the ring and formally asking JJ to marry him later that day. He just couldn't wait until New Years. Her adamant yes had everyone cheering, making toasts with hugs and kisses all around. Michaella took the question of the dual wedding right out of Dennis's hands by stating firmly that it would only make sense for them to make it so. She started ticking off the reasons on her fingers.

The men would be each other's best men. Both bridesmaids would be there. The invite list would be the same. The cost of venue could be shared and it would be more fun! Decision made; this was meant to be!

JJ was floored at how her friend had taken complete control of the situation and she just laughed along with the others. Sitting next to the man she loved, with a new family around her, she was a new woman and would never have to be that lonely little girl or woman ever again.

It really was strange how a dramatic event, such as she had just gone through, could change a person's life so completely. She was so grateful she had the forethought to ask for help from the only person she had called a friend.

Fate was on her side when Michaella showed up too with the only friend of her past. Not realizing what the one week during her teens had meant for her, JJ wondered if her mother would have approved of Dennis. Smiling, who wouldn't like him! He was a gentleman, a great uncle to his friends' children and a great buddy to his friends.

A nudge from Dennis brought her back to the conversation. She smiled up at him and around the room. Everyone had been watching, waiting for an answer, apparently.

Calmly, yet with a firm voice, JJ said, "I think it's a great idea! The sooner the better! And Michaella, I have thought about your business proposal and it's the best idea I have heard and would love to be your partner."

JJ stood and walked first toward Gage and Marlena, wrapped her arms around them in a hug thanking for the help and accepting her to their family. She then went to everyone else in the room, who had been there to help her, and in turn did the same to them. Lastly, JJ came to Dennis. With a gleam in her eye, she openly kissed him.

"You have all made me so happy! I can't wait to start this new part of my life; with the man I love and the new friends and now family!"

Dennis just smiled and knew he had found a jewel of a woman to make his future one any man would envy!

About the Author

Born and raised in Minnesota, Eleanor Jane resides with her husband, Jim, in central Minnesota. They have three daughters and one son-in-law. Some of her favorite hobbies are gardening, reading and spending time with her family. After acquiring a lake home, she enjoys the natural beauty of the lake and wildlife there. She loves nothing more than to watch the many varieties of migrant birds that come to her feeders, the wild turkeys, loons, swans and eagles, and deer. She started writing for herself a number of years ago, during a short period between jobs. Once her family learned of it, they encouraged her to have her works published. After her first book, **The Retreat**, was published, her readers asked for a sequel. It took Eleanor time to come up with the storylines for a sequel, she has done so with The Rescue and now The Relocation. She is developing the storylines for more to this series, so watch for them to come.

Books by Eleanor Jane

The Shadows Series
The Retreat
The Rescue
The Relocations

Stand Alone Novels
Elizabeth
An Overdue Healing

CPSIA information can be obtained
at www.ICGtesting.com
Printed in the USA
BVHW031100200619
551533BV00008B/214/P